The Italian Vineyard Mystery

Stitched in Secrets

K. L. Bordeaux

Ezra DiMarco

Copyright © 2024 by K. L. Bordeaux and Ezra DiMarco

All rights reserved.

No part of this book may be reproduced in any form or by any electronic or mechanical means, including information storage and retrieval systems, without written permission from the author, except for the use of brief quotations in a book review.

We can be found on all social media sites.

Be sure to read the rest of the series Stitched in Secrets. Follow Eliza and her special cat Merlin as they solve crimes all over Europe.

Chapter One

Eliza Bennett stepped out of the sleek taxi, her eyes narrowing against the brilliant Tuscan sun that cascaded sending liquid gold over the undulating vineyards. The landscape before her was a masterpiece waiting to be captured on canvas, if only her demanding career as a world-renowned textile scientist allowed such indulgences. Her expertise in the arena of fabric arts was coveted by industries and museums alike. Everybody wanted her for her discerning eye. She was capable of dating ancient tapestries with uncanny precision. It was this talent that had earned her an invitation to this luscious corner of Italy.

The journey from New York City had been relatively smooth, with just a brief layover in Frankfurt to break up the transatlantic flight. Now, as she gazed upon the verdant hills surrounding Siena, she smiled. Color had always been her joy, her raison d'être, and here, she felt a thrill. This, she thought, was truly living.

. . .

"You gonna let me out?"

Eliza jerked to a start. She leaned over and undid the latch to a pet carrier she had at her feet. Out stepped a discontent orange tabby cat with a hot air balloon-sized ego.

"Merlin, I was just admiring the landscape."

Her cat went with her everywhere. Of late she'd been on call to so many conferences, she'd almost lost count. Just last month they'd been in France. It was summertime.

"Do you realize where we are?" Eliza sang out. She stretched her arms wide in exaggerated awe as she spun in place, taking in the vibrant landscape. "Tuscany! Home of romantic sunsets and —"

"And surly wine makers," Merlin interrupted, his voice laced with sarcasm. He sprung gracefully to the top of a craggy stone wall, holding his tail high, defying the naysayers of feline decorum with every confident flick. "And let's not forget the family feuds. What could possibly go wrong?"

"Lighten up, fur ball," Eliza laughed. "It's an adventure! Think of all the fabric dye research we can do! Not to mention the exclusive vineyard tours..."

"Wonderful," he growled, fixing her with a glare that could wilt a vine. "Nothing I love more than flying grape juice. Are we seriously risking life and limb for color swatches?"

"Shh, Merlin. You know if I succeed here with my research here, I'll be considered for admission into The Society."

"Yeah, yeah. You've talked about them enough. So, if you get more money, how will that benefit me?"

She leaned over and whispered into his ear. "More catnip, my dear."

They turned to face the vine-smothered façade of

The Italian Vineyard Mystery

Calbretti Vineyard, a picturesque establishment oozing rustic charm. The heavy timber door creaked open, revealing a tall man with sun-kissed skin making him look like a golden raisin. He had a permanent scowl across his rugged face. Lorenzo Calbretti, the vineyard's self-proclaimed tortured artist of wine, was every bit the over-worked producer one would imagine.

"Can I help you?" he huffed.

"Actually, I'm Eliza!" she chirped. "Here for the dye research? I'll be studying how grape skins react with different solutions and swatches."

Merlin shot her a sidelong glance. Muttering under his breath, he added,"Yes, because nothing screams cutting-edge fashion like a bunch of fermented fruit stains. What's next? A dress designed for the next grape harvest?"

"You'll need to follow the rules around here, Miss Bennett. No gallivanting about my property. And"—he gestured toward the expansive vineyard—"stay away from the Rizzos. They're trouble. Want to end up as a new vintage? Because they'll have you bottling quicker than you can say 'interfering tourist.'"

"They sound delightful," Eliza replied. She punctuated her sentence with a fake laugh. But her enthusiasm remained. She and Merlin had read up on the Rizzo family was notorious for their fierce rivalry with the Calbrettis, practically the Kardashians of Tuscan wine. Nothing could be more intriguing than feasting her eyes on this fresh drama unfolding in person. "Love a good bit of rivalry! Adds flavor to life, don't you think?"

"More like rancid vinegar," Lorenzo grunted. He turned to sneer at the cat. "What's this?"

"My plus-one," Eliza said. "I already cleared him being here."

3

"Very well. You're in Room Three. Try not to break anything or attract the Rizzos."

As he walked away, Merlin stood up on his hind legs, delicately resting his front paws on her legs to whisper conspiratorially, "How do you feel about grossly exaggerated hospitality? I would've expected dancing villagers, serenades, and of course, finely honed insults for newcomers. What a jerk."

Eliza shot back, "Maybe he's in pain."

"Or hungover."

She patted Merlin on the back of his neck. It never was a good idea to stroke him all the way down his back. He sometimes got grumpier than usual and would display his temper with a quick swipe.

"Perhaps we should explore the vineyard now. We wouldn't want to miss our chance at tasting the finest refreshments. I hear wine flows like rain in Tuscany." Eliza clutched up her bags.

"Or like melodrama in this vineyard," Merlin added sagely, plopping down elegantly beneath a nearby vine, his belly facing the sun like a makeshift cat throne. "Charming place you picked for us, Eliza. Honestly, it screams deceit and poor decision-making!"

Suddenly, a figure hissed at them as a woman approached them.

Merlin jumped up. "Yow!"

The stranger walked with smooth but deliberate steps. Standing tall, exuding both authority and bemusement, was a woman with long, dark hair that flowed elegantly behind her and deeply tanned skin testifying to countless Tuscan days.

"I bet that's his daughter," Merlin hissed to Eliza.

Giulia, Lorenzo's daughter, approached them with a

The Italian Vineyard Mystery

steely gaze that could zap clouds on the foggiest of mornings.

"What are your intentions here?" she spat.

Eliza cleared her throat, ready to charm even the most treacherous of vineyard guards. "Just doing some research on fabric dyes and—"

"Is that so?" Giulia interrupted, crossing her arms tightly like a barricade. "My father and I don't take kindly to meddling outsiders. This isn't exactly an open invitation."

'Come on now," Eliza said, her voice a blend of innocence and mischief. "What's a little harmless research? Surely it's not as treacherous as the chasing off of pesky Rizzos? It could make for great conversation over a nice glass of wine!"

"Right, because treachery and drink make perfect companions," Giulia said, her expression still suspicious. "Where were you going?"

She pointed to the bag that Eliza held in her hand.

"I wanted to look at the vineyard some," Eliza said in a faltering voice. "Your guest cottage is across the way and we just wanted to get an understanding of the lay of the land."

"We're only honoring this visit because of The Society made a special request," Giulia said.

"Madam, we appreciate everything," Merlin piped up.

Giulia stared at the cat, with her eyes growing wider.

"Get used to it," Eliza prompted her. "Everybody has that reaction at first."

Merlin smiled at the young woman. Then he added, "You think you know drama? You just wait until the next family grape fight. I'll grab the popcorn."

Merlin exchanged glances with Eliza, amusement flickering in his emerald eyes. "Well, now we've established there's a family feud. May I suggest you find a seat for the coming drama? It could get messy. And I, for one, wouldn't want to miss it."

Eliza walked toward Giulia with confidence, her gaze unwavering. "I promise you, I have zero intention of meddling. I'm just here to conduct research."

Giulia remained unimpressed, folding her arms tighter until they seemed glued to her sides. "Research? Or just nosy? Make sure you keep your distance—especially from the Rizzos. They're worse than vermin."

"Oh, I can handle myself," Eliza declared, excitement igniting her words. "I'm used to dealing with people like the villainous Rizzos. Not that I've met them in particular yet! But isn't that the best part of a good story? Unraveling mysteries and charm?"

Giulia stared at her for a beat longer, possibly realizing that Eliza's spirited bravado might either be entertaining or a catastrophic disaster waiting to happen.

"We'll see," she replied, turning her back with an air of disdain "Don't say I didn't warn you."

As Giulia walked away, Eliza turned to Merlin,"Well, that was fun! Apparently, the Rizzos are a hot topic over wine, too."

"Let's hope our little adventure sticks to fermented grapes rather than fermented chaos," Merlin quipped, stretching out luxuriously before rolling into a compact ball of fluff.

Eliza waved off the notion. "Pfft! What's life without a little risk? Now, let's explore these vineyards. There's fabric dyeing to do and maybe, just maybe, some scandal-worthy grape shenanigans!"

Merlin groaned theatrically.

Chapter Two

When Eliza awoke in her quaint room at Calbretti Vineyard, the the outside world beckoned her. Dinner the night before had been a dismal affair. Neither the father nor the daughter had much to say. Each line she was able to get them to say was as difficult as though the pair were sitting for an exam.

Her cozy room smelled of old wood and fresh linen—a combination that felt incredibly welcoming yet oddly reminiscent of her grandfather's garage. She stretched, a yawn creeping its way out, and glanced at Merlin, who lounged carelessly at the foot of her bed, snoozing blissfully.

"Ready to make the most of our Tuscan adventure?" Eliza chirped, throwing off the warm blankets and hopping out of bed.

Merlin cracked one eye open, the other firmly closed as if he were contemplating the existence of breakfast from his dream realm. "If by adventure you mean traipsing through grapevines like a lost tourist in search of self-discovery, then yes. Count me in," he replied dryly.

Eliza chuckled as she rummaged through her suitcase,

pulling on a lightweight sundress adorned with colorful patterns, far from the earthy tones of actual grape skins—a perfect mismatch for the study she was about to undertake. She liked to dress more outrageously than her usual demure outfits that she donned as a college professor back in New York

"I'm off to get some samples, and you're coming along to supervise—because someone has to keep me out of trouble."

"Or guide you to it, perhaps?" Merlin said, flicking his tail as he rolled off the bed to land gracefully on his feet. "Lead the way, though I suspect the only rogue behavior today will come from you picking too many grapes. Heaven forbid we face legal repercussions from the Calbretti estate."

"Wouldn't be the first time I've been accused of grape thievery, that's for sure," she said winking, then headed toward the door,. Merlin kept up with her, exuding an air of begrudging eagerness.

The last remnants of dew and the vibrant greenery of the vineyard sprawled out before them—a sea of brightly colored vines, all beckoning for attention. Eliza inhaled deeply, the scent of ripe grapes tickling her nose. She grabbed a wicker basket that she had specifically asked her hosts to provide and marched out, determined to gather a healthy selection of samples for her dye research.

As they ambled through the rows of vines, Eliza took in every element of the vineyard. "Wow, could you imagine how different it is for them during the harvest season?" she wondered aloud, absently brushing her fingers over the plump grapes. "I've only ever read about it."

"While I don't have personal experience of grape harvesting, I imagine it involves a sweet amount of hard work followed by excessive drinking and regrettable decisions," Merlin replied, cleverly veiling his own distaste for manual labor. "Much like your ideas about love."

Eliza shot him a glance. "You're such a killjoy. Not everything revolves around romance, you know."

"Oh really? You sure about that?" Merlin twirled his whiskers on the spot like a tiny furry philosopher. "I just happen to see the shimmer in your eyes whenever you think about the dashing son of the surly wine maker."

"Dashing?" Eliza flushed slightly. "You're imagining things."

"Am I? I saw how you ogled him whenever he was in on the Zoom calls before we flew here." Merlin paused, his eyes sharpened "Let me remind you, it's not simply chemistry you're looking for in this vineyard. You might want to study some of that frenetic energy coming off the vines too. Or maybe attempt to keep your emotions bottled up like the wine in that cellar."

Before she responded, a voice pierced through the enchanting bubble they were in. "What's going on here?"

Eliza and Merlin heard somebody make their way through the vegetation.

Eliza spun around, heart racing, and found herself face-to-face with the irresistibly handsome Antonio Calbretti. His tousled hair and chiseled jaw sparkled in the soft light, and his rolled-up sleeves revealed arms that seemed almost unfair.

"Uh, just gathering samples for my research," she stammered, her cool facade crumbling under his captivating gaze.

Merlin, ever the opportunist, bounded forward, purring like a well-oiled machine. "Research? What kind? Figuring out how many crushes you can stack up on a vineyard owner?"

Antonio chuckled, clearly amused by the talking feline. "Well, this is a twist! Are you saying your cat has taken on the role of a love consultant?"

"Not a consultant—a love maven! And just a tip: if you want the real grape essence, you should steer clear of Eliza's toxic charm!" Merlin declared, stretching his front paws dramatically.

Eliza laughed, embarrassed yet charmed. "I should have known he'd tease me! I could use a sidekick like you!" She shot a sheepish glance at Antonio, feeling her cheeks heat up. Today, it was unclear whether the sun or the striking vineyard owner was causing her blush.

Antonio stepped closer, a mischievous spark lighting up his deep brown eyes. "Well, you should keep Merlin on a short leash then; he's quite the character. But in all sincerity, good luck with your research. We Calbrettis like to pride ourselves on grape quality, too."

"Plus, it wouldn't hurt to help out the vineyard in any grape-related venture. Think of the publicity," she replied eagerly, adjusting the basket at her side. "I'll grab samples and see what kind of dyes we can whip up from these beauties. I've been dying to try out some new colors. You know how it goes—fashion waits for no one."

Critical to her quest, Eliza needed to use actual vegetation to test from the ancient region itself. Only this would give her research the credibility to parallel what may have been the practice thousands of years ago.

"Oh, I can only imagine," Antonio said with a playful grin, his gaze flickering to the vibrant grapes around them. "Listen, if you're after the perfect color, you should consider testing the skins from the Rizzo vines as well in different stages of ripeness. We might have some great competition brewing."

The Italian Vineyard Mystery

For a brief while, the three of them walked along the rows in the vineyard. Eliza felt blissful she'd finally encountered the heartthrob. Merlin was dubious and Antonio was oblivious as to Eliza's state of mind.

"Yes! Lead the way, you wise bard of bottled grapes," she said, pantomiming a faux courtesy as the two set off towards the weathered building that looked like it could use a solid dose of fairy dust and a good cleaning.

As the pair ventured deeper into the grove, Eliza felt a familiar thrill of adventure bubbling inside her—a sensation she rather enjoyed. She nudged Merlin with her elbow and said, "You know, if we don't find anything today, we definitely need to make one of our infamous 'Gems of Tuscany' videos immediately upon our return to the States."

They rounded the end of one row and saw a small dog messing with something on the ground. As they got closer, Antonio let out a huge groan.

"Papa!" he wailed.

Lorenzo Calbretti lay before them, his neck was encased in a thick vine that had been tightened. A note was safety pinned to his cotton shirt.

The note read:

Death by what you love. Justice.

"Don't touch anything," Eliza cautioned Antonio, but it was too late. Antonio threw himself in to a kneeling position and immediately pulled the vine off of his father's neck. It was too late, of course. The man was dead.

Sobbing, Antonio clutched his dad's chest and began trying to do CPR.

"Stop," Eliza said. "You can't..." She could tell by the victim's pallor that he was long gone.

"We need to call the police," she said. She reached out

and touched Antonio's shoulder. "Antonio, did you hear me? Call the police."

Merlin had already begun casing the environment for clues. He sniffed in several odd places and peered up and down several rows, always coming back to Eliza after each pass.

"The body is cold," he mentioned to Eliza.

"I know," she said.

Just then, the Rizzo family's presence showed itself, as a sharp, unmistakable voice cut through the tranquil air. "Antonio! What mischief are you up to now?"

Simona Rizzo, matron of the Rizzo clan, stepped into view, forceful and commanding, with an assertive posture that kicked any notion of a peaceful morning right to the curb. "Are you absolutely certain you want to be courting trouble with the outsiders? I wonder if we should call in a family meeting, just in case you need to learn your manners."

"Ah, here comes the other half of the entertainment!" Merlin muttered under his breath, shading his eyes as if to watch with interest. "Let the theatrics commence!"

She walked closer to them with a curious look on her face.

"Simona, go away," Antonio moaned. He barely looked up and returned to embracing his father's dead body. "Get the hell out of here!"

Eliza steeled herself, trying to swallow the lump of anxiety slinking down her throat as Simona kept getting closer.

Antonio stood up abruptly and advanced on the woman who had long grey hair.

"We were just discussing grape samples," Eliza chimed, attempting to mask her nerves with a smile that probably

The Italian Vineyard Mystery

looked more strained than charming. "Antonio helped me with my research on dye quality." If it were possible for her to cover up the entire scene to give Antonio his peace, she would have done that.

Simona's eyes flitted between taking in the body of the dead patriarch and Eliza's face.

"Who the heck are you?" she asked, "and what is wrong with the signore?"

"Go away, go away," Antonio kept telling her.

"Signora?" Eliza said weakly. "There's been an accident. Can you call the police?"

Suddenly everything fell into place for the neighbor. She began backing away, almost stumbling.

Her face crumbled and her mouth opened up into a big "O." At the same time she reached into a pocket and tried to dial but got nowhere.

Merlin pawed Eliza gently. "Looks like you need to call them," he said. "She's too rattled."

Standing near Antonio and his fallen father, Eliza whipped out her phone.

"Antonio, please tell me—how do I dial the police around here?"

"112," he answered. "Oh God, we need to tell my sister."

"She's here, isn't she?" Eliza asked.

"Yes. Hardly ever leaves. This is really bad for the two of us."

Eliza held up her hand, indicating the emergency operator had picked up. She moved her phone closer to Antonio's face.

"Tell her," Eliza urged. "I don't speak Italian."

Haltingly, in between sobs, Antonio explained what happened.

Meanwhile standing at her feet, Eliza heard Merlin whisper, "Charming to see you, Simona."

By the time Giulia was informed and rushed to the scene, Eliza and Merlin had headed up towards the main house.

"I think I will call that one 'She-who-loves-to-cast-shadows-when-there's-no-sunshine-around," Merlin observed as Giulia ran past.

"Be quiet, Merlin. Not everybody is up to your moods," Eliza told him. "Especially now. Shut up. Can't you do that for once?"

Her cat was silent for almost a full fifteen seconds. She heard him clear his throat first and then answer her. "No."

Chapter Three

Eliza couldn't believe the turn of events. One minute she was happily gathering grape samples, the next she stood amidst a crime scene, the idyllic Tuscan vineyard now tainted with tragedy. Antonio's grief was a tangible presence, suffocating the air around them. The image of him desperately clinging to his father's lifeless body kept replaying in her mind, a cruel juxtaposition to the playful banter they'd shared just moments before.

As they neared the Calbretti villa, Eliza noticed the once-charming facade now felt like it loomed over them, its terracotta walls exuding an oppressive aura. A wave of nausea washed over her, a potent mix of shock, fear, and the overwhelming scent of crushed grapes lingering in the air.

Bursting through the door, Eliza found the villa's interior just as heavy and somber as its exterior. Dark, antique furniture filled the room, the air thick with the scent of aged wood and a lingering aroma of espresso, a stark contrast to the bright, sun-drenched vineyard outside.

"Signora Bennett?" a voice called out.

A woman in her late 50s, her face filled with worry

lines, emerged from a room down the hallway. Her clothes, though simple, spoke of understated elegance, and a pair of reading glasses perched precariously on her nose. This had to be Francesca, Lorenzo's wife and Antonio's mother.

Eliza offered a small, sympathetic smile. "Please, call me Eliza."

"Eliza," Francesca repeated, her voice tinged with a slight tremor. "Antonio told me you were there with him when it happened."

Eliza nodded, unsure of what else to say. Words felt woefully inadequate in the face of such raw grief. She couldn't even begin to imagine the pain Francesca must be going through.

Francesca wrung her hands, her gaze distant, lost in a world of pain only she could navigate. "He loved this vineyard more than anything. It was his lifeblood, his legacy." Her voice cracked, and she paused, struggling to regain her composure. "To think... to think he died here, amongst the vines he cherished."

Eliza reached out, hesitantly placing a hand on Francesca's arm. She felt compelled to offer a silent gesture of comfort, an acknowledgment of the shared grief that hung heavy in the air.

As if on cue, the sound of approaching sirens pierced the quiet murmurings of the house. The wail grew louder, a stark reminder of the tragedy that had befallen the Calbretti family. Francesca's shoulders slumped further, her face crumpling. The weight of her grief was simply too much to bear.

The arrival of the police brought with it a flurry of activity. Grim-faced officers swarmed the vineyard. Their presence transformed the once-peaceful landscape into a crime scene. Eliza watched from the villa's entrance, a silent

The Italian Vineyard Mystery

observer to the unfolding investigation. She felt a hand on her shoulder and turned to see Antonio, his face pale and drawn, his eyes red-rimmed and filled with a profound sadness that tugged at her heartstrings.

"They want to ask us some questions," he said in a hoarse voice.

Eliza nodded, offering him a reassuring smile. "Of course. We'll tell them what we know."

The questioning seemed to stretch on for hours, a blur of flashing lights, hushed whispers, and probing questions. Eliza recounted every detail she could remember, from the moment they stumbled upon Lorenzo's body to their inter- actions with Simona Rizzo. Antonio, though clearly distraught, remained composed, his answers measured and precise.

As the sun began its descent, casting long shadows across the now-desolate vineyard, the police finally concluded their initial investigation. Eliza and Antonio were free to go, but a shadow of suspicion lingered over the Calbretti estate. The police, though tight-lipped, made it clear that this was no accident. Lorenzo Calbretti had been murdered.

Exhausted both physically and emotionally, Eliza retreated to her room, the weight of the day pressing down on her. The events of the day replayed in her mind, like a macabre film reel she couldn't turn off. The image of Lorenzo's life- less body, the look of utter despair on Antonio's face, the chilling note pinned to the dead man's shirt—each scene seemed more disturbing than the last.

Merlin, ever perceptive of Eliza's emotional state, jumped onto the bed and nestled himself beside her, purring softly. His presence, usually a source of comfort and amusement, reminded her of the danger lurking within the vineyard's picturesque beauty.

"What have we gotten ourselves into, Merlin?" she whispered, stroking his soft fur absently.

Merlin, for once, had no witty retort, no sarcastic quip. He simply rubbed his head against her hand, his silence speaking volumes. They were no longer on a quest for colorful dyes and artistic inspiration. They were caught in a web of secrets, lies, and a murder that threatened to unravel the very fabric of the Calbretti family legacy.

Ss

The days that followed were a blur of hushed whispers, furtive glances, and a palpable tension that permeated every corner of the Calbretti estate. The investigation continued, the police a constant presence, their questions relentless, their suspicions growing with each passing day.

Eliza, torn between her desire to help and the gnawing fear that she was in over her head, found herself drawn deeper into the mystery. She couldn't shake the feeling that there was more to the story than met the eye, a hidden truth lurking beneath the surface of the seemingly idyllic vineyard.

Driven by a sense of justice for Lorenzo and a growing concern for Antonio, Eliza decided to do some investigating of her own. She started by revisiting the scene of the crime, meticulously retracing her steps from that fateful morning. The vineyard, once a place of peace and tranquility, now held an eerie silence, as if nature itself was holding its breath, waiting for the truth to be revealed.

Standing before the row of vines where Lorenzo's body

The Italian Vineyard Mystery

had been discovered, Eliza noticed something she had overlooked before. A small, almost imperceptible footprint, partially hidden in the soft earth at the edge of the vineyard. It was too small to belong to Antonio, and definitely not a man's shoe.

Intrigued, Eliza took a closer look. The print was faint, but distinct enough to make out the outline of a delicate, almost child-like shoe. It was a clue, a small piece of the puzzle that didn't quite fit. Who else had been at the vineyard that morning? And why had they tried to conceal their presence? The mark was as semi-circle. What kind of shoe would have made this?

Determined to uncover the truth, Eliza confided in Merlin, her loyal companion and confidante. "A child's shoe, Merlin?" Eliza contemplated. "What could it mean?"

"Perhaps a tiny accomplice?" Merlin suggested, his tone uncharacteristically serious. "Or maybe someone trying to mislead the authorities, throwing them off the scent, so to speak?"

Eliza nodded slowly, considering his words. It was certainly a possibility. But who would go to such lengths to cover their tracks? And why target Lorenzo Calbretti, a man who seemed to be more passionate about his grapes than anything else?

Chapter Four

Back at their cozy quarters, Eliza and Merlin ponder whether to pack up and abandon their scholarly pursuits in light of the recent murder. Merlin, channeling his inner feline philosopher, argued for staying put—after all, there's no way the universe could throw this much absurdity at them and require them to walk away, he said.

Eliza, swayed by her adventurous spirit and Merlin's persuasive purring, decided they must dig deeper into this peculiar vineyard intrigue. Back in the coziness of their quaint cottage that had weathered more than a few storms—and several questionable decisions involving wine tasting and cheese pairings—Eliza paced the room like a caged lioness. Well, more of a gazelle with a flair for the dramatic, for while she had the aptitude for an epic story, her recent encounter with a very real murder back in France had her feeling less like an action hero and more like a character in a morbid Disney movie. Her hair bounced with each step, catching the light, but it did little to ease the knot of unease twisting in her stomach.

The Italian Vineyard Mystery

"Can we talk about how this whole vineyard escapade might just fall into the category of 'nope'?" she blurted out to Merlin, who lounged on a plush armchair as though he contemplated life from the pinnacle of Mount Wisdom.

Merlin, a bespectacled owl of a cat who seemed to carry the burden of the universe's silly mysteries, stretched lazily across the sunlit room, his presence dominating the space. He curled up in a sunbeam, asserting his feline authority over every nook and cranny, reminding the world that he was the ruler here. After a few moments of supreme relaxation, curiosity got the better of him. He padded toward the window, his whiskers twitching with anticipation.

With a graceful leap, he hopped onto the windowsill and then onto the roof, surveying his domain. From his lofty perch, he edged to eavesdrop on two figures conversing just below. The humans were oblivious to his presence as they exchanged worried whispers about unseasonable events occurring in the vineyard.

From his perch on the sun-warmed slates of the portico, Merlin lounged in a lazy sprawl, his eyes half-closed as he soaked in the warmth of the afternoon sun. The scene below him was a tableau of sibling tension he had learned to recognize all too well during his reign as chief observer of family dramas.

"Giulia, you can't make all the decisions on your own! This is the family business we're talking about!" Antonio's voice became loud, accusing, and a little too shrill for Merlin's feline sensibilities. The tomcat's ears perked up, ready to eavesdrop on this juicy discord that was about to unfold.

Giulia stood with her arms crossed, unwilling to let her brother's outrage ruffle her feathers. "And pray tell, what decision would you make, Antonio? Play around at the club some more? Or maybe audition for a role in your own tragi-comedy?" Her words dripped with sarcasm, each syllable a precise jab aimed right at her brother's self-image.

Antonio's face turned a shade of red reminiscent of ripe tomatoes. "That's not fair, and you know it! I have a stake in this too."

"You? You have a stake in this business when your best skill is juggling drinks and charming the bar fillies?" Giulia interjected. "You think you can just skip in here, all tan and carefree, and suddenly have a say? Come on!"

At that, Merlin flicked his tail in approval. Giulia had a talent for disarming her brother with her barbed wit, and he admired her tenacity, sprawled out in nonchalant comfort as he listened intently.

"Well, someone has to do something about our crumbling empire, and it sure isn't going to be the sister who refuses to stop playing around with the 'Enochian Style' tea infuser set she bought last week!" Antonio shot back, his voice echoing off the granite walls with a ferocity that made Merlin's ears twitch.

"Excuse me for trying to better the family brand," Giulia said. "Better to serve trendy herbal brews than sit in a leather chair pretending to be Daddy 2.0. We both know you're good at looking the part but terrible at the whole 'decision-making' part of it."

"Says the sister who can't even decide on a flavor of ice cream without calling in a committee!" He laughed, though it was more of a bitter chuckle than anything resembling mirth.

"Look, what else can we do?" She rolled her eyes. "Should we hire a private investigator to find out who killed Daddy?"

"Now who's being melodramatic?" Antonio blasted. "I

The Italian Vineyard Mystery

thought we were just charting how to salvage the family name, not a police procedural. I don't know how you can even think straight with that tea kettle of yours whistling in the background."

Merlin's ears perked upright. Tea infuser discussions aside, the mention of a private investigator had his whiskers twitching with curiosity. His next nap would surely be filled with dreams of detective capers, tinged with the excitement of revelation.

Giulia sighed heavily, clearly exasperated. "Maybe you need to stop playing the innocent victim for once and realize how much chaos has followed you.You care more about your escapades than the business!"

"Oh, and I suppose you're going to install a stern 'Giulia Management' sign on the front door, too?" Antonio slung the words back at her, a hint of playful sarcasm creeping back into his tone.

"Only if it comes with a warning sign saying 'Enter at your own risk'—very fitting for a player like you!"

If Merlin had been human, he would have chuckled appreciatively, if only to lighten the palpable animosity that flowed between them. But alas, he was merely a cat—a seasoned watcher of human antics who could only soak in the absurdity surrounding him.

As the tension escalated, his gaze drifted lazily over the balustrade, contemplating a tactical retreat for a nap.

Merlin grew bored and retreated back to Eliza's room to report on the conversation he'd just heard. Eliza took it all in and scribbled some notes.

She looked up at her cat. "I really need to start doing some testing rather than analyzing all this family drama crap."

"Go for it," her best supporter agreed.

Eliza dug into one of her bags and pulled out a testing kit and brought it over to the sink in the room and set the basket of grapes nearby.

"Hold your nose," she advised as she applied a series of drops to each grape and recorded her observations.

Merlin rolled his eyes and found a spot in the furthest corner of the room to pretend he felt asleep.

"Better not be like what you did in the lab back at home last month." he advised as he closed his eyes.

"Oh shut up, Merlin. You always remember the worst."

Merlin perked his head up at that to counter her but stopped when he saw Eliza flicked her wrist, unrolling the small, well-worn canvas bag that held her custom testing chemicals. Each vial, labeled in her careful, almost artistic handwriting, gleamed with promise. Acids, bases, indicators —each had a distinct role in her grand experiment. Pulling out a simple, elegant dropper, Eliza chuckled. "Who knew dealing with grapes could feel more like preparing for a laboratory heist?"

She scoured the sink. It seemed simple enough—sink equals water, water equals happy scientist—but the quaint charm of the vineyard house wasn't without its quirks. The sink had seen better days, soap scum lingering in its corners like an unwelcome party guest. Finally she turned on the tap, and clear water gushed forth with a satisfying rush, Eliza shrugged off the residue of neglect.

"Perfect," she said with a giddy grin.

With the sink running, she laid out her precious grapes: a handful of the ripest, deepest-purple bunches she had scavenged. "You beauties are about to become the stars of the show," she declared, her voice a dramatic whisper as if addressing a crowd. "Prepare for your close-up."

The Italian Vineyard Mystery

"I sure hope you finally get your prize," Merlin said. "Seems like those Society people been stringing you along."

Eliza selected a grape and held it up to the light, examining it as an artist would a canvas. She pressed it between her fingers, reveling in the slight resistance followed by the burst of juice. "Juicy! Perfect to test for acidity. Let's see just how acidic you really are." With a flourish, she then dropped the grape into a small glass beaker, glancing over her shoulder to catch Merlin's expression. The cat watched with rapt fascination. She imagined him as the world's most endearing lab assistant, eager for the next step in their experiment-filled journey.

She reached for the first vial, twisting the cap off with a dramatic flourish. Inside was a vibrant, almost sinister-looking liquid—an acid indicator, glistening menacingly in the light. "A splash here..." She drizzled several drops into the beaker, the reaction immediate as the liquid sizzled and changed color—a vivid dance of hues from bright green to a punchy pink. Eliza gasped, her eyes wide. "Oh, you sweet grape, you're practically begging for more sugar! Let the world know!"

As she scribbled copious notes in her notebook—a collection of haphazardly organized observations piled atop sketches of grape clusters and half-formed ideas for future experiments—Eliza smiled. This was more than just chemistry; it was a glimpse into the soul of the vineyard and of ancient history. She was uncovering the nuances of flavor, acidity, and potential. Her research also tracked the daily temperatures of the region. She needed to know everything —rainfall, human interaction, pruning cycles, soil types, topography, age of the vines. Each note was a stepping stone towards something grander, and the weight of discovery exhilarated her.

"Take note, Merlin! This could revolutionize our knowledge of their dye process—perhaps even change the world!" Her voice dripped with mock grandiosity. "Napoleon may have had his cake, but I have my chemistry! I want to recreate exactly what they did in the past."

Merlin tilted his head, as if considering her genius. Eliza smirked. She washed a second grape in the running water, her movements fluid, like a dancer twirling gracefully across the floor. She was in her element, the kitchen fading away as she focused entirely on her task.

Next came the pH strips. She dipped one into the beaker, her fingers deftly maneuvering it like a seasoned performer. Eliza squinted, watching as the color shifted once more, her heart racing as it settled. "Six point five—the perfect balance!" she exclaimed, clapping her hands together with delight before jotting the result down before it could slip from her mind. "It's practically begging for a barrel! This could work, this really could... I know you can make all sorts of colors from mushrooms alone. Why not grapes, too?"

Chapter Five

Before she knew it, it was dinnertime. The aroma of rosemary and garlic infused the air, a testament to the family cook's culinary skills. The cook arranged a platter of roasted vegetables as Antonio poured a robust red wine for Merlin. The dining room table, set for four, awaited the last member of their unusual dinner party: Francesca, Antonio's mother.

"She's taking this harder than she lets on," Antonio said, sighing as he set down the decanter. "My father, despite everything, was the constant in her life."

Merlin, his emerald eyes shimmering in the candlelight, dipped his head in understanding. "Grief is a fickle beast, Antonio. Allow her time."

Eliza placed a comforting hand on Antonio's arm. "We'll be here for you, both of you, through all of this."

He offered her a grateful smile. "I appreciate that, Eliza. More than you know. By the way, I'll be occupied with family matters for the next few days, caught in the whirlwind of funeral arrangements and the settling of my father's affairs. The Calbretti family, despite their internal strife, always manages death well."

Their conversation was interrupted by the sharp rapping of footsteps on the porch, followed by a thunderous pounding on the front door. The housemaid, scurried to answer it, her expression a mixture of confusion and alarm. A moment later, a whirlwind in black leather burst into the dining room.

The woman, tall and slender, was clad from neck to ankle in a black catsuit that hugged her figure like a second skin. Her long, dark hair flowed behind her like a cape, framing eyes wide with a mixture of anger and grief.

"Antonio!" she spat, her voice sharp with accusation. "Why didn't anyone tell me about Lorenzo?"

Antonio, taken aback by the unexpected intrusion, rose from his chair. "Illya, please. Calm down."

"Calm down?" Illya shrieked, throwing her hands up in the air. "Your father is dead! I had to hear it from Gina, the hairdresser, who heard it from the florist, who heard it from God knows who! Nobody thought to tell me?"

Antonio pinched the bridge of his nose, trying to quell the rising tension. "Illya, this is my home, and you do not barge in here and..."

"This is bullshit!" she interrupted, her voice echoing in the shocked silence. "I deserve some respect, damn it! Your father and I..." she trailed off, her anger momentarily eclipsed by a flicker of something vulnerable.

Antonio, sensing an opportunity for de-escalation, reached for his phone. "Giulia," he said, his voice tight with urgency. "Come down to the dining room immediately. We have a situation." He hung up without waiting for a reply.

Eliza, ever the picture of composure, addressed their

unexpected guest. "Signora, perhaps we could offer you some wine?"

"And who is this marvelous figure of fitness?" Merlin said gently, his tone laced with amusement.

Illya whirled around, her eyes widening as they landed on the talking cat. "Ugh," she groaned. "A talking cat. Just what this night needs." She turned back to Antonio, her anger reignited. "Your father promised me a stipend, Antonio. I expect you to honor that."

Antonio stared at her, his patience wearing thin. "A stipend? For what? For being his companion?"

"For what?" Illya scoffed. "What else? dsdFor being his whore? Let's not mince words, Antonio. I know my role."

The air crackled with tension. Before Antonio could respond, the sound of hurried footsteps echoed from the hallway. Giulia appeared in the doorway, her face pale with concern, dragging a hesitant Francesca behind her.

"What's going on?" Giulia asked, her gaze darting between Antonio, the furious Illya, and the stunned faces of Eliza and Merlin.

Francesca, her eyes red-rimmed and her face drawn, seemed to shrink further into herself. She clutched a handkerchief in her hand, her knuckles bone-white.

Illya turned to Giulia, her eyes blazing. "Your father promised me a stipend," she declared. "A monthly allowance to ensure my... discretion."

Giulia's jaw dropped. "What? Papa promised you money?"

Antonio, his voice low and dangerous, stepped forward. "She's lying," he stated flatly. "My father would never—"

"He did!" Illya cried, her voice cracking. "He promised! We had an agreement!"

Francesca, who had been unnervingly silent, suddenly spoke. "It's true," she whispered, her voice barely audible.

The room went silent. All eyes turned to the grieving widow. Francesca, her frail shoulders slumping under the weight of their gazes, continued, her voice trembling. "Lorenzo... he had been seeing her. For years. He gave her money, gifts. He said it was to help her, to get back on her feet. So she could train more horses once again."

Giulia stared at her mother, her face a mask of disbelief. "Mama, is this true?"

Francesca nodded slowly, tears welling in her eyes. "He swore me to secrecy," she whispered. "He said it meant nothing, that it was just a dalliance."

Illya, emboldened by Francesca's confession, crossed her arms over her chest. "So you see," she said, her voice laced with triumph. "Your father made a promise. And I intend to see it kept. I need money to buy at the horse auction next week. That's just for starters."

Antonio felt anger, hot and potent, course through his veins. His father, even in death, continued to cast a long shadow over their lives, dredging up secrets and sowing discord. He opened his mouth to unleash his fury, but Giulia stopped him, placing a restraining hand on his arm.

"Wait, Antonio," she said, her voice surprisingly calm. She turned to Illya, her expression unreadable. "You said Papa promised you a stipend. Do you have any proof of this agreement?"

Illya hesitated, her confidence faltering for the first time. "Proof?" she echoed. "We didn't exactly have a written contract, if that's what you mean."

Giulia nodded slowly. "So, you have no letters, no messages, no witnesses to corroborate your claim?"

The Italian Vineyard Mystery

"It was understood," Illya insisted, her voice taking on a desperate edge. "He promised me!"

"I understand," Giulia said, her tone clipped. "But unfortunately, without any tangible evidence to support your claim, this becomes a matter of your word against ours. And given the circumstances..." she let the sentence hang in the air, her meaning clear.

Illya's face flushed crimson. She opened her mouth to retort, but no words came out. She looked from Giulia to Antonio, her anger giving way to a flicker of fear.

Antonio, watching the play of emotions on Illya's face, felt a strange mixture of anger and pity. He knew his father well enough to believe that he was capable of such a callous betrayal, both of his wife and of Illya.

He stepped forward, his voice firm as he addressed Illya. "Look," he said, "I understand you're hurting. And you feel like you're owed something. But you need to understand, my father left us in a difficult position. Things are tight right now, undecided."

He gestured towards the dining table, where the remnants of their dinner sat untouched. "We're grieving. We're trying to pick up the pieces. And frankly, dealing with this situation is not high on our list of priorities."

He pulled out his wallet and took out several bills, extending them towards Illya. "This is all I can offer you tonight. It's enough to get you by for a while. But I suggest you find another source of income, because this ends here."

Illya stared at the money in his hand, her face a mask of humiliation. She wanted to refuse, to demand what she believed was rightfully hers, but the steely glint in Antonio's eyes told her that it would be futile.

She snatched the bills from his hand, her fingers

brushing against his palm in a gesture that was both intimate and resentful.

"Fine," she spit out, her voice thick with unshed tears. "But don't think this is over, Antonio. Your father made me promises. And I intend to see them kept, one way or another."

She turned on her heel and stormed out of the dining room, leaving behind a heavy silence. Eliza and Merlin exchanged uneasy glances, while Francesca sat frozen in her chair, her face pale and drawn.

Giulia broke the silence, her voice trembling slightly. "Mama," she said softly, "are you alright?"

Francesca looked up, her eyes filled with a lifetime's worth of pain. "I... I need a moment," she whispered, her voice choked with emotion. "Please, just give me a moment alone."

And with that, she rose unsteadily from her chair and made her way slowly out of the dining room, leaving her children to grapple with the wreckage of their father's lies and the secrets he had left behind.

Chapter Six

The following morning dawned over the Calbretti Vineyard with a fresh energy that crackled in the air like static before a storm. Eliza Bennett stood alongside Antonio, Guilia, and Inspector Mario beneath the shade of an ancient olive tree, plotting their next moves in the investigation that had spiraled out of control faster than a runaway gondola.

"So," Inspector Mario began, scowling, "we've gathered some information from the cellar, but we need to investigate further into Lorenzo's dealings. We need to consider all angles — including the Rizzo family's involvement."

"Great, let's just stroll over to their vineyard and ask for their secrets, shall we?" Eliza replied, sarcasm lacing her words. "I'm sure they'll be thrilled to share their trade secrets, right after they invite us for tea."

Merlin chuckled.

Antonio crossed his arms. "I'm all for a good fencing match. The Rizzos do love their theatrics. Maybe we should challenge them to a friendly competition — like grape jousting. Winner takes the secrets, loser serves as mulch."

Guilia turned to her brother, her demeanor both engaging and enigmatic. "While that sounds delightfully absurd, we must tread carefully. The Rizzos are like a bad case of indigestion — they'll turn on you quickly. Hey, look, I need to get on a business meeting. Can you all handle this?"

"Sure," Antonio said.

"Indigestion and grape jousting in one breath? How do you come up with this?" Eliza asked, unable to keep from giggling.

"Just brainstorming the possible future outcomes of this investigation," Antonio replied, leaning towards her as if conspiratorial. "Who knew sleuthing could be so adventurous?"

Merlin coughed. "I do."

"Adventure is one thing, but mystery is another," Mario interjected, glancing around the vine-stretched landscape as if it held the key to rich secrets lurking among the grapes. "We need to gather evidence, and that begins out here. Let's split up and check the vines for anything suspicious. Look for a torn or cut stalk."

With that, they agreed to separate into groups. Eliza teamed up with Antonio, happy to spend more time alone with him. As they walked side by side among the grapes, the air thick with the scent of ripe fruit, Eliza felt Merlin bump against her leg. She looked down at him and he gave her a thumbs down and shook his head.

"We'll need to keep our eyes peeled for anything," Antonio said, pointing to a row of vines that seemed to tremble unnaturally in the breeze. "Perhaps an odd sign? Or maybe a Rizzo plotting behind a bush?"

Eliza smirked. "Hopefully no enemies lurking nearby. That would be just our luck, wouldn't it?"

The Italian Vineyard Mystery

"You mean like those two over there?" Antonio said, nodding toward a cluster of individuals just beyond the trellis — none other than two Rizzos, brazenly whispering amongst themselves. "Didn't I tell you about the grape catastrados?"

"Grape what?" Eliza asked, eyes wide in mock confusion.

"Grape catastrados," Antonio continued with an exaggerated emphasis. "The calamities that befall us when rivalries spiral out of control. Much like this," he gestured toward the Rizzos, emphasizing theatricality, a grin stretching across his face.

"Ah yes, our very own sitcom unfolding right before us. It may even beat the reality shows back home!" Eliza laughed.

"Careful, our sweet sitcom could suddenly turn into horror if you don't watch it," Merlin muttered.

Merlin fluffed his fur, allowing his shameless attitude to manifest fully. "I hardly mind being an observer! Have you considered how intriguing it would be to document your downfall?"

"Just what I need—a feline as my life coach!" she declared with a playful sigh, turning her attention back to Antonio, who was stifling a laugh.

Eliza then led them toward the vines, searching for anything unusual. As they moved through the dappled sunlight, she felt the warmth of Antonio's presence behind her.

"Here," she said, shining her eyes over clusters of grapes, "look at this batch—it seems larger than the rest!"

"That's because they're being coaxed into overproduction," Antonio remarked, inching closer. "We've been having trouble with that ever since my padre's... demise. Watery grapes do not lend themselves to quality wine."

A disturbance in the rows of vines caught their attention as Eliza stepped forward. "What if there's...?"

Before she could finish her thought, a sudden rustling erupted from behind them, followed by the sharp laughter of the Rizzos.

"Look who's busy rummaging around the prize-winning grapes!" Simona Rizzo emerged, flanked by her brother, a smirk plastered across her face. "A couple of amateurs trying to sniff out secrets? How adorable."

"Amateurs don't usually have the charm you possess, Simona," Antonio shot back, his tone light but defensive. "But nice to see you're taking an interest in the family competition—or should I say, familial disaster?"

"Let's just say when Calbrettis are poking their noses where they don't belong, it resurfaces as a certain..." Simona's expression twisted and she let her words die in the air.

Eliza exchanged glances with Antonio, sensing the tension bubbling like fermenting grapes. "We're merely examining what's left of the vineyard. No big secrets here," she asserted confidently, doing her best to project strength.

Merlin jumped on top of a post so he could be eye level with Simona. Then he hissed.

"Oh darling," Simona replied, her tone dripping with condescension, "secrets are what make life fascinating. Especially when they involve family feuds and hidden debts among our vineyards. Your father still owes us."

Antonio stepped closer to Eliza, sharing an almost imperceptible look of solidarity. "It's a wonder you haven't gone through Lorenzo's papers more thoroughly, then — don't you think?"

The Italian Vineyard Mystery

Simona eyes flashed. "We'd only dig into dirt if it spelled 'dirt' for your family. Now, if you'll excuse us—there are more important matters at hand."

With a curt nod, she turned on her heels, her brother following suit, leaving Eliza and Antonio standing in the wake of the unpredictable tension.

Antonio rested a forearm on the border fence between their two properties.

"What on earth was that all about?" Eliza asked, exhaling deeply.

"Welcome to the Tuscany rollercoaster!" Antonio replied. "You should've seen that coming with an invitation like that. They're experts in deflecting."

"What started the feud?" she asked.

"Genetics," he told her. They stole some of our stock.

They ventured deeper into the vines, determined to uncover any clues they could while the sun warmed their backs. While wandering, they stumbled upon traces of crimson splatters on the ground—remnants of grapes crushed beneath careless feet.

"Perhaps a clue?" Eliza knelt to get a closer look. "This looks suspicious!"

"True. Normally we collect all our grapes and don't let them hit the ground."

Merlin padded up beside them, eyes sparkling with cleverness. "Big, small—it's all a matter of perspective. Either way, we wouldn't want to miss the grand finale of this soap opera, would we?"

Just as Eliza opened her mouth to respond, a sudden rustling emerged alongside them, and a startled butterfly fluttered past, only to take flight in panicked arcs. Then came a sharp gasp— not a butterfly, but a sudden shadow looming behind them, cloaked in a presence they hadn't anticipated.

"What's this? Trouble brewing again in the vineyard?" came the voice of the figure.

"What now?" Eliza muttered, turning to face what was causing her heart to pitter-patter.

As the figure emerged, she realized it was none other than Inspector Mario again, casting a shadow as he prepared to drop another bombshell.

"I found something else," the inspector said. "Antonio, do you recognize this? I found in the North field."

Antonio examined a gold watch that Mario handed to him.

"It's my dad's."

"Thought so. We found it by the steps to your main residence. Perhaps there was a struggle there? And we see hoof prints. Do you know why?"

"My father had taken up horseback riding late in life. Those are probably old. He prided himself on riding the rows sometimes," Antonio explained.

Eliza's heart sank as she caught the frantic expression that flashed on Antonio's face. "So there really was a struggle?" she asked.

Inspector Mario nodded gravely. "It appears so. We need to piece together what happened. This"—he gestured with the watch—"could be a critical connection to what transpired last week."

Antonio's fingers grazed the scratched surface of the watch, and memories flooded his mind. "But how did it get there?" he murmured, nearly to himself.

"Perhaps it fell during the altercation? Or—" Eliza paused. "What if he was meeting someone? Someone from the Rizzo family?"

The Italian Vineyard Mystery

"It could explain their arrogance," Antonio said. "If they're hiding something, then we need to bring it into the light before it's too late."

Merlin sniffed the ground, his whiskers twitching with interest. "My whiskers rarely lie. We should investigate that path leading to the house. It might yield something more tangible."

"Agreed," Eliza affirmed. "But first, let's examine what we can around here. There might be more evidence."

As they returned to the spot where they'd found the watch, the situation transformed the vineyard into something foreign—no longer a sanctuary of sunlight and grapevines but a complex tapestry of betrayal and shadows. Eliza spotted uneven footprints beside the crushed grapes, a trail that suggested hurried steps, perhaps left by someone desperate to escape.

She pointed to the ground. "Look—do you see that? Those tracks lead away from the house toward the fence line."

"Could be a getaway route," Antonio speculated.

Merlin expertly bounced into the air, landing gracefully beside the print. "This is turning into quite the treasure hunt! Adventure awaits, and we must seize it before it slips through our paws!"

Chapter Seven

The group of Inspector Mario, Antonio, Eliza and Merlin the cat ended up at a dead end at a fence line although they where facing the Rizzos' property.

"Huh," said Antonio. "Typical that that all roads lead to the Rizzos'."

The inspector shrugged and said, "I intend to question them more closely soon. The fact that you just buried your father and everything else that's going on over here leads to a lot of confusion. So far they have refused to talk to me."

Before she could stop him, Merlin dashed in a blur of orange under the fence.

"Where are you going?" she called.

Merlin answered,"I'll be back in a few."

Antonio put his arm over the Inspector's shoulder. "Care to join us for lunch, Inspector? I'll get Guilia to come down."

. . .

40

The Italian Vineyard Mystery

Merlin slinked towards the Rizzos' house, his fur barely touching the ground as he pressed onward toward the Rizzo property. The faint sound of Antonio inviting the Inspector to lunch faded as he navigated through tall grass and around garden decor, his agile form hidden from view. Muffled snippets of conversation from the yard grew louder until he reached an open window, nestled among the tendrils of a creeping ivy.

He crouched low, perfectly out of sight, his ears twitching forward to capture the dialogue within the dimly lit room. Simona Rizzo stood near a vintage oak table, her dark eyes flashing with fervor as she spoke to her brother, Rocco. Her arms were in constant motion, her gestures painting invisible pictures of outrage mid-air.

"I'm telling you, Rocco, those Calbretti people are nothing but trouble," Simona fumed, her voice tinged with both anger and frustration. "I don't understand why anyone even gives them the time of day."

Rocco, a tall, burly figure with a face sculpted by shadows, frowned deeply. He leaned back against the wall, arms crossed as he listened to his sister. "Isn't that a bit harsh, Simona?" he said cautiously. "What have they ever done to us?"

"What haven't they done?" she retorted, pacing back and forth. "First, they try to muscle in on our business territories. And then, there's this whole mess with Lorenzo. You know what they say about the Calbrettis, Rocco—the grape doesn't fall far from the vine!"

Merlin's ears perked even higher at the mention of the Calbrettis' father. His whiskers quivered with curiosity as he took in each word, careful not to miss a syllable. He was keenly aware that any scrap of information could be crucial in piecing together the tangled mess his friends were trying to unravel.

Rocco sighed, running a hand through his short, dark hair. "Look, we need to be strategic about this. Bad-mouthing them in public won't help our position. If anything, it'll just set us up for more conflict."

"But Rocco," Simona began, only to be cut off by her brother's upraised hand.

"No 'buts,' Simona. We need to play this smart. Keep your friends close and your enemies closer, right?" Rocco reasoned, his tone brokering no argument. "Besides, Inspector Mario is already sniffing around. We can't afford any slip-ups."

Simona bit her lip, clearly torn between her smoldering anger and the practical advice her brother offered. She finally slumped into a nearby chair, her eyes still simmering but her body language defeated. "Fine, but I'm not happy about it. And mark my words, one way or another, we will deal with the Calbrettis."

With that, Merlin's ears picked up the sound of foot-steps heading towards the door. Merlin decided it was time to make his retreat before being discovered. He silently slinked away from the window, retracing his steps with nimble ease until he was safely back under the fence and out of sight.

When he emerged on the other side, Eliza rushed forward, relief mixed with annoyance in her eyes. "Where have you been, Merlin? What did you find out?"

"Plenty," Merlin purred, his tail flicking with satisfaction. "And trust me, you'll want to hear every word of it."

Chapter Eight

Merlin sauntered along with them, his fur slightly ruffled from his latest outdoor adventure. He perched himself on the windowsill, curling his tail regally around his paws as if preparing to make an important announcement. His green eyes glinted as he fixed his gaze on the humans.

"I heard some interesting things next door," Merlin remarked, his voice tinged with a feline air of mystery.

Inspector Mario, standing by the coffee table, let out a sigh and shook his head after heard what Merlin had to say. "That's all well and good, Merlin, but without something concrete, it won't get us anywhere. It's time to get serious with the investigation."

Just then, Inspector Mario's phone buzzed loudly in his pocket. He fished it out and answered the call, his expression growing serious as he listened. He hung up and turned to Antonio.

. . .

"I'm sorry, but I have to leave. We'll have to take a rain check on our lunch plans," Mario said regretfully.

Eliza and Antonio exchanged glances before deciding to continue their walk up the hill to the main house, with Merlin trotting behind them like a silent, four-legged shadow. The path wound through lush greenery, the sun casting dappled shadows on the ground.

As they walked, Eliza finally broke the silence. "How long has Illya been involved with your father? And what does she do for a living?"

A pained expression crossed Antonio's face. "My father took a fancy to her a while back. Suddenly, he was insistent on learning to ride a horse, despite his age."

Eliza raised an eyebrow. "So, she's an instructor?"

Antonio nodded, a mixture of frustration and amusement in his voice. "Yes. My mother knew from the start what was going on. He was acting like a different man—always smiling, strutting around like he was ten years younger. It became an open secret in no time."

He paused, a sigh escaping his lips. "My poor mother."

They reached the crest of the hill, where the grand house loomed before them, its walls soaked in history and secrets. Merlin, ever the curious cat, meandered around them, occasionally darting into the bushes and re-emerging like a fish flashing among the currents.

"So Illya teaches horseback lessons?" Eliza asked, piecing together the information.

"Yeah, she's quite well-known around these parts," Antonio confirmed.

Eliza frowned. "And why does she think you all owe her money?"

Antonio's face darkened slightly as he struggled to choose his words carefully. "Well, my father assured her

The Italian Vineyard Mystery

he'd provide for her, to make sure she was financially secure. I guess it was his way of gaining her trust and convincing her to stick around, despite the complications of his marriage."

Eliza nodded thoughtfully. "So he made her promises to keep her close, even if that meant bending the truth a little."

"Exactly," Antonio agreed. "It's caused a lot of tension, and now she feels we're obligated to keep those promises, even though the situation is a lot more complicated than my father made it out to be."

They reached the grand entrance of the main house, and Antonio pushed open the heavy wooden door. Merlin darted inside first, his nose twitching as he sniffed the air.

The house was a blend of old-world elegance and modern conveniences, with high ceilings, antique furniture, and the faint smell of lavender. Eliza glanced around, taking in the grandeur.

Antonio's voice broke through her thoughts. "I hope you understand a bit better now. It's a mess, but I'm trying my best to sort it out."

Eliza smiled reassuringly. "I get it, Antonio. Family dynamics are rarely simple. What's important is that you're making an effort."

Merlin sprung onto a nearby armchair, sprawling out comfortably. "They say curiosity killed the cat, but in this case, it might just solve a few mysteries," he chuckled.

Eliza laughed softly. "Let's hope so, Merlin."

Ekiza looked at Merlin. "We need to do some more testings. If you'll excuse us for now." Eliza and Merlin left.

.   .   .

That evening Eliza and Antonio were in the middle of an intense discussion about the intricacies of vineyard management when the sound of a bell reverberated through the large estate. It was a clear, crisp chime, unmistakable in its purpose. The cook was calling them down for dinner.

Eliza's face brightened, welcoming the break. "Time to eat," she said, standing up from her chair and smoothing out the wrinkles in her dress.

Antonio nodded, running a hand through his dark hair. "It's about time. I'm starving," he grinned.

As they descended the wide oak staircase, the aroma of roasted chicken, herbs, and freshly baked bread filled the air. They walked down the hallway adorned with family portraits, remnants of a rich history now shadowed by tragic events.

When they reached the dining room, Guilia was already there. Her face appeared drawn, eyes shadowed by stress and annoyance. She barely acknowledged their arrival, her fingers tapping anxiously on the table.

Merlin, with an uncanny ability to sense emotions, prowled the room. His brilliant orange figure darted between chair legs and table corners. He gave Eliza a particularly piercing look, as though trying to communicate something crucial.

Eliza glanced back at Merlin. "Is everything alright, Guilia?" Eliza asked, taking a seat opposite the woman.

Guilia sighed heavily and pressed her palms against the table. "No, everything is not alright," she said.

Antonio settled beside Eliza, placing a comforting hand on her leg. The dining table, with its glossy mahogany surface and lace tablecloth, seemed almost a mockery of the tension hanging in the air.

Merlin's green eyes fixed on Eliza, and he began

The Italian Vineyard Mystery

rubbing insistently against her other leg, his alert posture signaling a warning. Eliza reached down, giving the cat a gentle pat, trying to soothe him while simultaneously attempting to interpret his message.

"What's gone wrong?" Antonio asked, concern etching lines into his usually calm face.

"The—" Guilia started but had to pause to collect herself. "A lot of our orders have been canceled. Because of Father's murder." Her eyes filled with tears, which she angrily brushed away.

There was a beat of silence, heavier than any filled with words. Antonio's grip on Eliza's leg tightened slightly, possibly in sympathy or reflexive worry. Eliza felt a wave of discomfort, but couldn't muster the strength to brush his hand away.

"Is there anything we can do to help?" Eliza asked softly.

Merlin jumped onto the table, knocking over the salt shaker, causing everyone to look at him. He walked purposefully to Eliza and sat before her, tail wrapping around his paws, his eyes feeling like they were boring into her soul.

Guilia looked at Merlin and then back at Eliza, her expression slightly puzzled. "That cat always seems to know more than he should," she said, her tension easing just an iota.

Antonio leaned closer to Eliza, his breath warm against her ear. "Don't you think it's odd that a cat can sense so much?" he murmured.

Eliza resisted the pull to become too absorbed in Antonio's proximity and instead focused on Guilia. "We'll figure something out."

Merlin, seemingly frustrated by the lack of immediate response to his warnings, began to walk over everyone's plates, disrupting their neatly set cutlery. Guilia swatted him away, a faint smile trying to break through her gloom.

"Alright, alright, Merlin. Message received," Eliza said, finally removing Antonio's hand from her leg gently but firmly, and instead intertwining her fingers in her lap.

Antonio shrugged, a look of mild disappointment on his face, but didn't press further. Instead, he turned his attention back to Guilia. "Cancellations are hard, but it's not the end. We can weather this storm."

"It's not just the cancellations," Guilia said, taking a deep breath. "People are talking—rumors spreading about our family, gossip that's killing our reputation."

Eliza frowned. "What sort of rumors?" she asked, feeling Merlin's supportive warmth now by her side.

Guilia hesitated for a moment, eyes darting to the closed doors as if fearing eavesdroppers. "Some are saying Father was into illegal activities, and that his death was some form of retribution."

Antonio banged his hand on the table. "That's absurd," he said, face darkening with anger. "We need to set the record straight."

The cook entered, oblivious to the tense atmosphere, to serve the food, placing steaming dishes in the middle of the table. The smell was inviting, but no one reached for covered dishes.

"I've already contacted a PR firm. They're helping us with a statement to counter these disgusting rumors," Guilia said, exhaling slowly, the weight of exhaustion evident.

"That's a start," Eliza said, thinking through ways they could further mitigate the damage. "Perhaps you could host an event—something that shows your commitment to the community and proves your integrity."

Guilia's eyes brightened slightly. "That's not a bad idea,

The Italian Vineyard Mystery

Eliza," she said. "We could showcase our new wine line, invite the press, and local leaders."

Antonio nodded, finally reaching for a slice of bread. "Let's do it. We need to fight back with dignity and transparency."

As everyone started to eat, Merlin settled contentedly beside Eliza, purring softly—a signal that at least something was beginning to fall into place.

"It's about time," Merlin whispered to Eliza.

"Merlin seems satisfied with our plan," Eliza remarked, giving the cat a gentle scratch behind the ears.

Guilia managed a true smile this time. "Cats always know, don't they?" she said, finally starting to eat as well.

"Yes," Eliza replied, "though sometimes their methods of communication are a bit unorthodox."

Antonio leaned back in his chair, looking thoughtful. "What if we also invited some of our major clients to the event? Assure them personally that our operations are completely above board and unaffected by recent events."

"That's a good strategy," Guilia conceded. "Face-to-face interactions often have the most powerful impact."

Merlin sat there, tail flicking with satisfaction, and Eliza felt a glimmer of hope for the first time in days.

Chapter Nine

The Calbretti estate began organizing a large banquet.They hired the best in the business at Guilia's urging. Eliza and Merlin tried to stay out of the way because of all of the commotion. Every day caterers now brought in tables and crates of food. The Calbretti son and daughter decided to open one of their older wine cellars for the event. It amused Merlin to see all the humans rush about. That was the exact opposite of the way he liked to live his life.

One night Antonio paid Eliza a visit in her quarters. Merlin was insistent that he stayed between the two of them. He wouldn't let Antonio lay a hand on her.

"What do you think you're doing?" Eliza asked Merlin when Antonio left.

"I'm protecting you," her cat answered.

"Protecting me from what?" Eliza retorted, crossing her

The Italian Vineyard Mystery

arms in defiance, the glow of an oil lamp casting soft shadows on her face. "Antonio is just being polite, and besides, we both know he has no intentions beyond pleasantries."

"Harumph, pleasantries."

Merlin flicked his tail, a gesture that betrayed his possessiveness. "It's not the intentions I concern myself with, but rather the implications. He's a Calbretti, and though his charm is evident, his lineage carries weight—and with it, potential dangers. I don't like that man."

Eliza sighed, sinking onto the plush chair beside her writing desk. "You have to trust me, Merlin. I can handle myself. This isn't a fairy tale. It's not like every prince has a dark secret lurking beneath his handsome facade."

"But if it were?" Merlin inquired, his golden eyes glinting as if brooding over his own tale. "What if you discovered that the rollicking laughter of this upcoming banquet hides whispers of intrigue, perhaps even betrayal? After all, the finest wines can sometimes contain the bitterest poisons."

Eliza leaned back, pondering the weight of his words. "So, you believe I should just lock myself away, swathed in caution and paranoia? Is that how you plan to protect me, Merlin?"

· · ·

"No," he replied, his tone softening, "But I would rather you be wary than careless. The world spins faster when you dance among shadows."

Just then, a knock at the door. When she opened the door, there stood Antonio again, an enigmatic smile playing on his lips, as though he had just stepped out of a grand novel.

"Eliza," he began, his voice low and inviting, "the preparations are nearly complete. I thought you might like a sneak peek at the wine selection we've curated for the banquet."

Merlin's ears perked up, and he settled himself in the doorway, blocking the entrance ever so slightly.

"Thank you, Antonio, but—" Eliza started, a flicker of hesitation in her eyes as she glanced back at Merlin, who narrowed his gaze.

"But?" Antonio pressed, cocking an eyebrow, the charm thickening around him like honey. "It would be a shame to miss out on the beauty of a vintage sourced from the very soil of this estate. Surely, you'd want to be part of that history, wouldn't you? Plus it might give you more depth for your research."

The allure of adventure sparking a conflict within her. "I suppose I could take a quick look," she finally agreed. Yet, she felt Merlin's disapproval radiating across the threshold like an icy blast.

The Italian Vineyard Mystery

. . .

"Just remember," her cat warned her in a whisper low enough for her to hear, "beneath every carefully curated bottle lies more than just the promise of flavor."

With a reluctant exhale, Eliza stepped past Merlin, who huffed in resigned frustration, appearing to settle back on her bed with an air of unease. She followed Antonio down the dimly lit hall. The distant murmuring of the preparations hummed behind them like an ancient song full of secrets and shadows.

As they entered the cellar, the air shifted, cooler and dense with the scent of aged wood and damp earth. Rows upon rows of bottles glistened in the dim lighting, each one whispering its own story. "Here," Antonio said, pulling out a bottle with a flourish, "this is the Crown Imperial. It's said to elevate any gathering, but it also carries with it the stories of those who drank it before."

"What do you mean?" Eliza asked, searching for the truth hidden beneath his smile.

Antonio leaned in closer, his voice barely above a whisper. "Legends tell of lovers united and friendships betrayed over this very wine. The laughter shared is often accompanied by the echoes of those who didn't find their way home."

. . .

53

He leaned in for a kiss. Eliza sidestepped away.

Eliza's pulse quickened as she sensed the weight of his words. "And you believe this will enhance our banquet?" she asked, pretending to take in the label of another bottle that she picked up.

He chuckled softly, a sound that reverberated around the stone walls. "Not merely enhance, dear Eliza; it has the power to transform the very atmosphere. A joyous celebration can turn into something deeper—feelings laid bare and alliances tested."

For a fleeting moment she visualized the two of them together in a tryst on her nice soft bed. "Is that what you intend, Antonio? To test the loyalties of those gathered?"

He turned away, focusing on pouring them each a taster. "Not my intent, but I cannot predict how fierce the tides of emotion may run once the bottle is uncorked." He handed her a glass. "Taste this and savor it the way it was meant to be, my love."

"Love?" she questioned. "I barely know you."

"Doesn't matter." He winked and poured her some more.

He placed the bottle on the thick wood table before them, a gesture as light as air yet heavy with significance.

. . .

The Italian Vineyard Mystery

Merlin, who had followed them stealthily, watched from the shadows, thumped his tail impatiently. Yet, he mostly remained still, keeping his head low as he observed Eliza through hooded eyes. Would she heed the subtle warnings in what Antonio said or throw caution to the winds and become entranced by the allure of the playboy?

With a sudden resolve, Eliza turned to Antonio. "There's a darkness lurking beneath the festivities then, isn't there?"

Antonio's handsome face broke into a broad smile. He lifted his eyebrows and teased her. "Every celebration holds its secrets, Eliza. To dance amidst them is to embrace life in all its chaos. You must decide how you wish to partake."

As the tension swirled between them, Eliza felt the weight of her choices pressing down. She glanced back toward the entrance, suspecting Merlin was nearby.Still, there was a thrill in the unknown, a beckoning towards the winding paths of the evening.

"Can I ask one favor?" Eliza started. "If we are to share stories, let's not do it in whispers or shadows."

Antonio regarded her for a moment, surprise flickering across his face before he nodded. "Very well, Eliza. Let's raise our glasses to honesty and transparency."

. . .

As they both reached for a bottle, the world outside continued its frenzied preparation. Little did Eliza know, the night held more than mere wine and laughter.

With the bottle cradled in her hands, Eliza sensed the weight of history resonating within the glass—yet, it was not simply the vintage that intrigued her. It was the knowledge that once uncorked, the air would thrum with unspoken words and the potential for revelations.

"Let's go back up," she suggested. "We should present this to everyone at the soirée, not keep it hidden down here."

Antonio's smile widened, revealing his calculated amusement. "Ah, the fearless adventurer awakens! Very well, let the others taste the nectar of confession!" He pulled out a few more bottles from the same row.

As they ascended the stairs, the murmur of revelry grew louder. Yet, a lingering doubt tugged at Eliza's thoughts— had she unearthed a source of excitement, or had she merely opened a doorway to rivalry and resentment?

Merlin, now trotting behind them, felt the shift in tone. Reading the energy of this dark man plagued him. He desperately wanted to deter Eliza from making the wrong choice. "Do be cautious, dear Eliza," he meowed softly, his

The Italian Vineyard Mystery

tail undulating softly as they broke through the upper level. "Curiosity sometimes lures you into the darkest of corners."

The guests spilled from the grand hall out onto the main portico and all over the outside of the main house. The entire area was alive with chatter and laughter, the glittering chandeliers and torches cast a magical glow over the guests in their finest attire. As Antonio and Eliza entered the scene, heads turned, appraisingly gauging the newcomers with a mixture of curiosity and expectation.

"May I have your attention, please?" Antonio called out, his voice cutting through the din as if he were born for the spotlight. Eliza stood a step behind him, feeling the weight of all eyes upon her.

"Tonight, Eliza and I have discovered something extraordinary," he continued, raising one bottle high. "A vintage that promises not just to delight, but to evoke the very essence of friendship and loyalty untested."

Eliza took a steadying breath. She started to think that maybe she had had too much to drink.

But this was her moment to shine—to turn the tide against the unseen currents of manipulation.

.   .   .

"And in the spirit of openness," she interjected, her voice stronger than she felt, "let us not only indulge in this wine but also in the honest exchange of thoughts and stories tonight."

A murmur rippled through the crowd, some faces brightening with anticipation, others flickering with skepticism. Eyes lingered on her.

"Here's to unveiling truths!" Antonio proclaimed, his gaze lingering on her, as if challenging her to match him word for word in this delicate game.

"To unveiling truths!" echoed the crowd, glasses raising with a clink that reverberated like whispered conspiracies. Yet behind the raucous laughter, Eliza felt a pulse of tension. It was as if each clink concealed a story waiting to unravel.

A server approached with a silver tray full of clean empty glasses. Each glass begged to be filled with the mysterious, potent wine, at least if Antonio had anything to do with it. He immediately began pouring.

Eliza caught Guilia's eye.

"Who are all these people," Eliza asked Guilia, indicating a large knot of people clustered around a bar counter in one corner of the room.

"Ah, all the big families of the region are represented tonight," Guilia answered. She nodded to crowd, all familiar

The Italian Vineyard Mystery

to her. "Look we have the the stoic Weavers, the charming Tanzi, and lurking in a corner, the enigmatic Giselle. These are not merely guests; they were potential allies or adversaries draped in the finery of their wealth."

Antonio deftly poured the deep crimson wine, the liquid flowing, filling each glass with what felt like promise and peril. Then he ceremoniously nodded to the server. "You may go," he said.

Merlin prowled about the edge of the hall, his ears perked and eyes narrowed. With every sip taken, he absorbed the shifting allegiances in the room, feeling the weight of unspoken words simmering amongst the laughing crowds. Old rivalries became new again.

Uncharacteristically, Eliza raised her glass and belted out, "Let's toast."

"Here, here!" the guests cheered, their spirits lifted in the shared revelry.

Merlin shook his head. To him, the air pulsed with uncertainty.

As the glasses touched, Eliza felt a tingle of electricity course through her.

Chapter Ten

Merlin surveyed the crowd a few hours later. The humans were getting sloppy drunk. What he witnessed now reminded him of the famous painting by Hieronymus Bosch. Merlin had personally seen that triptych The Garden of Earthly Delights at the Museo del Prado in Madrid during one of Eliza's ventures there. At this party now, women draped themselves over men. Dirty plates lay everywhere because the waiters could not keep up. Everyone had gotten way too happy. This is gross Merlin thought. A cat would never allow things like this.

Suddenly Francesca stood on top of the stairs and banged a couple pans together to draw attention. The crowd became silent.

"Thank you for coming to commemorate my late husband's life." She threw up her arms and banged the pans again over the top of her head. Eliza was entranced to see the older woman so animated.

"It must be the wine," Merlin chuckled to Eliza.

The Italian Vineyard Mystery

"Indeed," Eliza whispered back.

Francesca lowered her arms and became more serious. "I also thank you for allowing us to introduce our new wines." A loud cheer erupted from the crowd.

She paused, dipping her head. Eliza watched as the woman composed her thoughts.

"Although many times I detested my Lorenzo, he was still the love of my life."

With that she broke down crying and Antonio had to help her away.

Merlin frowned and muttered, "Silly human."

Eliza gave him a warning nudge with her foot.

After he returned to his spot next to Eliza, Antonio kept putting his arm around Eliza's waist. He'd done this several times during the evening but Eliza was moving about so much she kept slipping through his arms. One reason she did keep moving away was each time Antonio made an amorous advice to Eliza, Merlin quietly sank his claws in to his owner's ankles.

Francesca regained her composure after Antonio led her back to a table, swiping a hand across her tear-streaked face. She attempted to smile, raising her glass high. "To love, to loss, and to new beginnings!" she shouted, her voice gaining strength as she forced bravado.

As another cheer erupted. Merlin felt the weight of the revelry tightening around them, heavy and chaotic.

The music swelled again, a lively tune that beckoned couples to the dance floor. Merlin considered the folly of humans—caught in their emotional disasters as they spun across the stone floor of the porch, arms flailing and laughter echoing, oblivious to the impending disaster of their revelry. So very un-catlike.

Antonio dipped low to whisper something sweet into Eliza's ear. Merlin's fur bristled, but he maintained his steadfast gaze on the far wall, stoically imagining the graceful arc of a cat leaping unfazed from one serene perch to another, far from this pandemonium. Oh, if only he could leave this mess.

Francesca, seizing the moment, sang an impromptu ballad, her voice quivering with emotion, rich and poignant. The crowd swayed, entranced by her vulnerability, a wave of empathy washing over the intoxicated throng. Now that? That was difficult for Merlin to ignore the beauty of the moment—the connection amidst the chaos.

Still, he could not help himself. With a whip of his tail, he gave Eliza's ankle a particularly sharp swat, a reminder that the exquisite simplicity of a cat's existence was far superior. She winced, shooting him a withering look.

As if sensing the change in atmosphere, the music slowed, and couples began to intertwine in an affectionate dance.

Francesca, with her glass raised high, joined Antonio, who offered a hand.

Merlin felt conflicted. He had an undeniable longing; a gnawing desire to leap into their playfulness, to feel the

The Italian Vineyard Mystery

warmth of camaraderie whirling around him like a tempestuous wind. Yet the yearning was quickly flaked away by a niggling unrest. He curled his tail tightly around his paws—and sulked.

"See, Merlin, we're having fun," she told her cat.

"It looks too crazy for me," he told her.

Chapter Eleven

Eliza grew weary. The air buzzed with the lingering thrum of the festival, a discordant harmony of fading music and the distant echoes of laughter. Eliza, her head throbbing slightly from the day's festivities, leaned against a gnarled olive tree, watching the last embers of the bonfire die down. The scent of roasted garlic and sweet, smoky wine lingered in the air, a tangible reminder of the debauchery that had unfolded earlier that evening.

She took a sip of the mineral water she carried in a vintage Italian travel flask, the chill served as a welcome comfort against the lingering warmth of the Tuscan night. Her gaze drifted to the sprawling vineyards, the rows of vines standing sentinel against the darkened sky, their dark silhouettes a reminder of the Calbretti estate's success.

"They call it the Nectar of the Gods," a voice drawled knowingly beside her. "I'm back from taking care of my mother. My sister is nowhere to be found. Typical."

Eliza turned to see Antonio his dark eyes sparkling in the moonlight. His perfectly sculpted features were softened but the playful glint in his eyes remained.

The Italian Vineyard Mystery

"It was a memorable celebration," Eliza replied. She had been impressed by Antonio earlier that day, his charm and easy laughter drew her to him.

"Indeed," Antonio said, stepping closer, his hand reaching out to lightly brush a stray lock of hair from her forehead. "But I have yet to taste the true nectar of the Gods."

His gaze lingered on her lips, the implication clear. Eliza's pulse quickened, a spark of intrigue flickering to life. Antonio was a captivating man, undeniably handsome, and she couldn't deny the allure of his playful advances.

"You already have," she countered, her voice a playful whisper. "It's in the grapes, the soil, the very air here."

Antonio laughed, a low, rumbling sound. "You are a woman of mystery, Eliza," he whispered, his voice laced with admiration. "A true scientist, delving into the secrets of nature."

Eliza blushed, the warmth spreading down her chest. "It's just research," she replied, trying to maintain a semblance of composure.

"Research that certainly got my interest," Antonio declared. "And research that deserves a proper celebration. May I, perhaps, offer you a tour of the estate's hidden gems tomorrow?"

Eliza hesitated, intrigued but wary. Antonio exuded an almost tangible aura of seduction, his charm as potent as the finest vintage wine. "I am here to study the grapes," she finally replied, a hint of firmness in her voice. "My research is paramount."

There, perched on a low-hanging branch of the olive tree, sat her companion, Merlin. Antonio noted the animal's almost unnervingly intelligent expression. He stared at

Antonio with blatant disapproval, his fur puffed up like a miniature thundercloud.

"Merlin, please," Eliza muttered, hoping to soothe her feline companion's apparent discomfort. "We're just talking."

The cat's gaze didn't waver. He simply sat there, his tail twitching ominously.

"My, my," Antonio said, his voice coolly amused. "A jealous admirer, I see. Don't worry, my dear Eliza," he said, his hand reaching out to gently stroke the cat's fur. "There's plenty of affection to go around. You're certainly not the only one who finds me fascinating."

Suddenly, with a surprising display of feline agility, Merlin leaped from the branch, landing on Antonio's shoulder with a soft thud. He arched his back upwards, his claws extended, and let out a menacing hiss.

"Merlin!" Eliza exclaimed.

Antonio yelped, stumbling back, a look of surprise and even a hint of fear on his face. The cat, surprisingly vicious for such a small creature, attacked Antonio with ferocious intensity, raking his face with its claws.

"Get off, you damn beast!" Antonio yelled, his voice filled with fury. He swatted at the cat, his hands landing on nothing but air. Merlin, with an incredible display of agility and balance, continued to attack, his small, sharp teeth nipping at Antonio's skin.

Eliza, realizing the situation had spiraled out of control, hurried to pull Merlin off Antonio. "Merlin! Stop it! That's enough!" she shouted, her voice ringing with authority.

The cat reluctantly complied, his small body trembling with barely-contained rage. He leaped back onto the olive branch and sat there, his green eyes glinting with a sardonic amusement.

The Italian Vineyard Mystery

Antonio, clutching his face, staggered back, his eyes wide with a mixture of shock and anger. He looked at Eliza, his expression contorted with hurt and betrayed. "You knew," he spat, his voice a venomous hiss.

Eliza felt a sinking feeling in her stomach. She knew, even without Merlin's apparent psychic abilities, that Antonio was a charmer, a player. But she had allowed her own desires to cloud her judgment.

"No," she replied, pleading. "I didn't know."

Antonio scoffed, his injury apparently forgotten in the face of his wounded pride. "Don't play the innocent, Eliza. I see through you, just as clearly as I see through your little friend."

He glared at Merlin. "He knew," he said, his voice dripping with scorn. "He knew all along what you were. And now he's exposed you for the fraud you truly are."

Eliza's face burned with shame and confusion. She had no idea what to make of the situation, of Antonio's venomous words, or Merlin's unusual behavior. The cat, inexplicably, seemed to be assume an almost human persona, his actions a reflection of some deep-rooted psychic intuition.

"I'm not a fraud," she said, her voice trembling with anger. "And Merlin did not know you before all this."

Antonio nodded, his smile unwavering. "Of course, of course," he said, his voice smooth as velvet, suddenly changing tact as he dabbed at his face. "But even a dedicated scientist deserves a moment of relaxation. Let me attend to my wounds. And I expect you to help me with that." He turned on his heel and left.

"Good riddance," Merlin spat.

Antonio walked to stand at the edge of the now-quiet courtyard, a half-smile playing on his lips as he watched the twinkling lights of a departing car disappear down the cypress-lined drive. The last of the guests had gone.

His eyes fell on the guest quarters nestled among the vines. It was there that Eliza, the striking textile scientist from New York, was staying. She had come to Calbretti with that awful unusual traveling companion, Merlin, a large, opinionated feline with an uncanny ability to sense the unseen. Eliza was here not just for the wine, but to delve into the history of the land, to extract the ancient secrets of dyes from the very grapes that had made the Calbretti name famous across the world. He picked up a bat to carry with him.

Next he adjusted his crisply tailored suit, a signature of his playboy lifestyle, and made his way toward Room Three, where Eliza was likely to be readying herself for bed or poring over her notes and samples. The night still throbbed with the scent of blooming jasmine and the distant hoot of an owl. Antonio felt a familiar thrill. He was a man accustomed to getting what he wanted, and Eliza, with her sharp intellect and exotic beauty, was his latest desire. So far, she'd been putting him off. He dabbed at his face with a handkerchief and began humming.

As he approached the room, he heard the soft strains of classical music mingling with the evening breeze. He knocked lightly on the door, his smile widening as Eliza opened it, her eyes bright with surprise, then darkening with slight suspicion guilty .

"Ah, Signorina Eliza," Antonio purred, his gaze sweeping over her. "I hope the festival was not too much of a distraction for your important work. And I need help with these scratches, please."

Eliza's eyes softened at the sight of him, the flush of the evening's excitement still coloring her cheeks. "Not at all,

The Italian Vineyard Mystery

Antonio. It was quite the spectacle. Your winery certainly knows how to celebrate. Yes, I'll doctor you up.

Antonio chuckled, stepping closer. "And what of you, Eliza? Have you found what you're looking for in our humble vines?"

"I've only just begun," she replied. "The grapes here hold a history I intend to unravel. I already have found many color spectrum in the skins."

As they spoke, Merlin appeared from the shadows, his green eyes fixed again on Antonio with an unsettling intensity. The cat sprung onto the Eliza's writing desk, flicking his tail with disapproval.

"And how is your feline companion?" Antonio asked, trying to mask his unease. Merlin was no ordinary cat, and his presence was a constant reminder that not all was as it seemed in the world of the living.

"Merlin is well, thank you," Eliza said, reaching out to stroke the cat's sleek fur. "He's been quite helpful with my research."

Antonio's eyes lingered on Eliza, his thoughts shifting from small talk to the true purpose of his visit. "I was hoping, Eliza, that I might see you here in your room. It's quite late, and the paths can be treacherous in the dark. Just ensuring your safety."

Eliza hesitated, her gaze flitting between Antonio and Merlin. The cat's warning growl was low but clear, and she knew better than to ignore it. "That's very kind of you, Antonio, but I assure you, I'm quite capable of locking my own door. Let me dress your wounds and then we can both retire for the evening."

Antonio's smile didn't waver, but there was a new intensity in his eyes. "Humor me, Eliza. It would give me peace of mind to know you're safely inside after we do the cleanup." He nudged his way against the door.

Antonio stepped closer, his voice dropping to a husky whisper. "Eliza, I must confess, it's not just your mind that intrigues me. There's a magnetism about you that I find irresistible."

Eliza's heart fluttered, but before she could respond, Merlin hissed, his eyes flashing with an otherworldly light. He jumped onto Antonio's back, his claws digging through the fine fabric of his suit.

"Merlin!" Eliza gasped, trying to pull off the enraged cat. "I'm so sorry, Antonio!"

Antonio stumbled forward, shock and pain etched across his face as he fought to dislodge the feline assailant, dropping the stout stick he'd brought with him. "Madre di Dio!" he cursed, his composure shattered. "What the devil has gotten into this beast?"

Merlin's growls grew louder, his fury unabated as he thrashed wildly. Antonio, desperate to regain control, reached for Eliza, trying to ensnare her in an embrace that was more trap than comfort.

"Eliza, stay back!" he commanded, his voice laced with panic. "I won't hurt you, but this cat is mad!"

Eliza's mind raced, her eyes wide with alarm. She could see the headlines now: "Playboy Vintner Mauled by Psychic Cat." But beneath the absurdity of the situation, a cold realization settled over her. Antonio's charm, it seemed, was merely a veneer, hiding a core of selfishness and entitlement that she had failed to see.

With a strength born of desperation, Eliza managed to pry Merlin off Antonio, holding the still-growling cat in her arms. "Antonio, you should go," she said firmly, her voice

The Italian Vineyard Mystery

cutting through the chaos. "I think it's best if we forget this ever happened."

Antonio, disheveled and shaken, straightened his suit, his pride wounded more deeply than his flesh. "Yes, perhaps that would be for the best," he murmured, his eyes avoiding hers. "I apologize for my enthusiasm. It won't happen again."

Without another word, he turned and walked swiftly away, his retreating figure swallowed by the darkness. Eliza watched him go. She turned to Merlin, who had finally settled down, his piercing gaze fixed on the path Antonio had taken.

"Thank you, Merlin," she whispered, burying her face in his fur. "I think I owe you one."

Later, as Merlin sat on her desk cleaning his claws, some tiny hunks of the fabric of Antonio's suit fell onto her blotter. Eliza brushed them aside to a corner of her desk. She was busy working on her iPad answering emails but noted the multicolor strands of the expensive clothing.

"Hmm," she mused to herself. "I wonder if this is silk?"

She snapped her iPad shut, leaving the questions of the day unanswered.

Chapter Twelve

The morning sun, already warm through the burgeoning grape leaves, seemed to mock the chill in Eliza's bones. She watched from her room a strange scene. It appeared the entire vineyard staff and surrounding community was there. Antonio mounted a borrowed chestnut mare. His face, usually open and welcoming, was a mask of grim determination. He held a length of thick grapevine in one hand, its raw end trailing in the dust.

Beside him stood Giulia, his younger sister, her face pale and drawn. Their mother, Francesca, a woman who normally exuded an air of quiet strength, seemed to shrink within herself, clung to Giulia's arm.

Antonio addressed the crowd. Eliza saw Inspector Mario among the group. From her veranda she could hear his voice amplified in the stillness. "After my father's brutal murder," he began, his gaze sweeping over them, lingering a beat too long on Illya, the riding instructor, "I swore I would find the truth, no matter how painful."

Illya stood stiffly, her face carefully blank, but Eliza,

The Italian Vineyard Mystery

who had befriended the woman, saw the flicker of fear in her eyes. Beside her, Merlin let out a low hiss, his fur bristling. He had been agitated since Antonio announced his "demonstration."

Eliza chose to walk down and join the group.

"I discovered something," Antonio continued, his voice taking on a dramatic tremor. "The murderer, in their haste, left behind a clue." He held up the vine. "This is no ordinary vine. It's from the north field, where my father's watch was found. And," he paused, letting the tension coil tighter, "it was used to drag his body."

He gestured sharply and a burly vineyard hand, his face pale and set, was dragged forward. The man stumbled, tripping on the rough ground.

"And now we demonstrate."

Antonio kicked the horse forward. The noose tightened around the worker's neck and the man yelped in pain.

"This could only have been orchestrated by somebody who knew my father well and who my father trusted. Plus had the strength to manage an animal as large as a horse." Antonio's voice rang out. He looked pointedly at Inspector Mario, resplendent as always in a crisp linen shirt and tailored trousers, who stood with arms crossed, a contemplative frown on his face.

Eliza, felt a surge of anger and a strange certainty that this was all staged. Merlin tensed beside her. He pressed against her legs, a low growl rumbling in his chest.

"Antonio," Eliza called out, her voice cutting through the hushed spectators. "May I examine that vine? As a textile scientist, I might be able to tell you more about it."

Antonio hesitated, a flicker of annoyance crossing his face. "This is a matter for the police, Signora," he said, but before he could continue, Giulia spoke up, her voice thin but insistent.

"Let her see it, Antonio. What harm could it do?"

Her brother, after a beat of tense silence, nodded curtly. "Inspector Mario?"

Mario, eyebrows raised in curiosity, waved a hand. "By all means, Signora. Let us see what your science can uncover."

Eliza, heart pounding, knelt beside the vine. Picking up the rough length, she saw, woven between the dried bark, tiny, almost invisible fibers. They were multi-colored, she realized with a jolt, just like what she'd seen the night before in her own room.

She looked up, meeting Mario's eyes. He was staring at her, his face unreadable.

"I need to examine these fibers more closely," she announced, her voice firm despite the shudder in her chest. "Inspector, may I borrow this evidence for further analysis at the station?"

The air crackled with tension. Beside her, Merlin purred, a low rumble of satisfaction vibrating through her. Antonio's expression became a turbulent ocean of defiance and reluctance. "You want to take evidence away? This is a vital part of the investigation!"

Giulia stepped forward, her small stature belying the fierce protectiveness in her voice. "If it helps find out who really killed our father, then yes. Let her do it."

Eliza spoke up. "It doesn't have to leave police custody."

Inspector Mario remained impassive, as if weighing the merits of their pleas against the backdrop of the assembled crowd, who had shifted uneasily. Eliza sensed the collective discomfort—the thirst for justice tempered by a deep-seated fear of what they might unearth.

The Italian Vineyard Mystery

"Fine," Mario finally stated, his voice cutting through the murmur like a knife. "But you must ensure that nothing is tainted. I had the inspector do this as a special favor, Signora. Evidence holds the key to truth, and I cannot afford any missteps. Isn't that correct, Illya?" He sought out Simona Rizzo. "And you Signora Rizzo? You hated my father just as much."

Illya only scowled and didn't say a word. Simona Rizzo spat on the ground.

With a swift nod, Eliza accepted the vine from Antonio, the coarse texture rough against her palm as she clutched it tightly.

"Thank you," she said evenly, meeting Antonio's intense gaze. "We'll find the answers." She handed it back to Mario.

As she turned to leave, Eliza felt a prickling sensation at the back of her neck, making her hairs stand on end. She glanced back once more; Antonio was watching her intently. It thrilled and unnerved her in equal measure.

Eliza asked Antonio, "What do you know about the north field?"

As she turned to re-join the crowd, she noticed Giulia standing with her mother, looking over the gathered group. There was innocence lingering in the woman's expression, yet behind that innocence, a flicker of awareness sparked. It was as if Giulia understood the unfolding fabric of their lives was woven with sinews of darkness and light, mystery and truth. Some pieces had yet to fall into place.

"But what of your life?" Guilia asked. "There are those who would rather keep their secrets buried than face the repercussions. You meddle with delicate strings, Eliza, and you risk unraveling the tapestry of our world. Tread carefully."

Eliza felt a strange threat from the woman. They were

both piecing together fragments of a fractured puzzle but Guilia preferred to keep things closed.

Just then, a loud gasp rose from the crowd, drawing her attention. Antonio had stumbled slightly off the mare, his face having drained of color. He gripped the saddle tight, his knuckles white as if bracing against an invisible storm.

"The North field!" he suddenly shouted. "We need to ride there! Now! There's bound to be something still left—something my father wouldn't have willingly left behind!" He grabbed Eliza and threw her up into the saddle, then mounted behind her.

"Antonio, wait!" she called. "You—"

He cut her off abruptly. The intensity of his grip pinned her momentarily. "We will find what they tried to hide! My father deserves justice!"

"Justice is not served by recklessness!" Eliza shot back, breathlessly. "If you rush into it like this, it could lead to more chaos! We need a plan. We should gather evidence, not just act on a whim."

But Antonio's mind was made up. Without further delay, he shouted over into her ear, "We ride!" And before she could protest further, he urged the mare forward. The chestnut took off with an urgency unmatched by any horse Eliza had ever been on.

Giulia moved to join them. "Wait for me!" she exclaimed. She ran after them yelling, "I'm coming!" Guilia rushed to catch the mare's tail as they began their descent towards the north field but that was in vain. The sister was soon left behind.

Eliza tried to look back to see if Merlin was near but Antonio forced her face to stay forward with one hand.

As they galloped through the verdant rows, the air filled with the pungent scent of earth and ripening grapes. Eliza

The Italian Vineyard Mystery

tried to make sense of what Antonio had done to her. It was only by her experience with horseback riding that she managed to stay on. Vines whipped her legs.

They reached the edge of the North field, an area shrouded in eerie silence. The world beyond was untouched, leaves fluttered with an unspoken tension. This appeared to be a neglected part of the vineyard. Antonio quickly dismounted and pulled her off.

"We look. We look for clues," he huffed, his eyes roving like a madman's.

Merlin caught up with her, panting. "Why did you leave me?" he spat.

"I couldn't stop the horse," she lied.

Chapter Thirteen

The North field was a tapestry of neglect, a stark contrast to the meticulously maintained rows of the main vineyard. Twisted vines clawed at the sky, their leaves withered and brown. The air hung heavy with the scent of decay, a cloying sweetness that spoke of forgotten harvests. Antonio, his earlier fervor replaced by a grim determination, led the way, his eyes scanning the ground, searching.

Eliza, slowly recovering her breath, followed closely, acutely aware of the vulnerability of her position. The imposing cypress trees that lined the perimeter of the field cast long, skeletal shadows, twisting familiar shapes into ominous silhouettes. She couldn't shake the feeling of being watched, of unseen eyes following their every move.

Merlin, his senses on high alert, padded silently beside her, his orange fur blending seamlessly with the dappled shade and dying leaves. Occasionally, he would let out a low growl, his teeth bared in a silent snarl, sensing something she couldn't.

"Antonio," Eliza whispered, her voice barely audible

The Italian Vineyard Mystery

above the rustling of the wind through the dead leaves, "What exactly are we looking for?"

Antonio paused, his gaze sweeping across the desolate landscape. "Anything," he muttered, his voice tight with suppressed emotion. "Anything my father might have left behind. A message, a sign, something to point us in the right direction."

Eliza wanted to believe him, to share in his conviction that they would find answers here, but doubt gnawed at the edges of her mind. The North field felt more like a dead end than a source of truth, a place where hope withered and died.

As they ventured deeper into the heart of the field, the oppressive atmosphere pressed in on them, suffocating. The ground beneath their feet was uneven, littered with fallen branches and thorny weeds that snagged at their clothes. The silence was broken only by the crunch of their footsteps and the distant, mournful cry of a bird.

Suddenly, Antonio stopped so abruptly that Eliza bumped into him. He stared at something on the ground, his eyes wide with a mixture of horror and grim satisfaction.

Eliza followed his gaze and gasped. Partially hidden beneath a tangle of dead vines lay a small, leather-bound book in a plastic bag. Its once-bright cover was scratched and faded, but even from this distance, she could see the initials embossed in gold on the front: "L.C.."—Lorenzo Calbretti, Antonio's father.

Antonio carefully knelt down, his movements almost reverent, and gently picked up the book. He brushed away the dirt and debris, revealing more of the cover. The gold lettering was tarnished, but still legible. It read: "My Legacy: Secrets of the Calbretti Vineyard."

"This," Antonio whispered, "This is what they wanted to hide."

Eliza's breath caught in her throat. She could feel the weight of the book, the potential secrets it held, like a physical presence. This was no ordinary journal; this was a Pandora's Box, and she had a feeling that opening it would unleash a storm that would change the Calbretti lives forever.

"Antonio," Eliza began, her voice hesitant, "Are you sure you want to do this? What if—"

"There's no 'what if,' Eliza," Antonio interrupted, his voice resolute. "This is my legacy too, and I need to know the truth."

With that, he opened the book. The pages, yellowed and brittle with age, crackled in protest. The first few pages were filled with neat, flowing handwriting, documenting grape varieties, pruning techniques, and weather patterns. It was a meticulous record of a life dedicated to the vineyard.

As they turned the pages, the entries became more personal, filled with thoughts, dreams, and anxieties. Antonio read aloud, his voice trembling with a mixture of grief and anger.

"They were stealing from him," Antonio breathed, his face pale with shock. "The Rizzos, the foreman, even some of the villagers... they were all in on it. Skimming profits, selling our grapes under a different name. They were bleeding my father dry."

Eliza's heart went out to him. To have his father's legacy tarnished like this, to discover such betrayal within his own community. It was almost too much to bear.

As they delved deeper into the journal, a chilling pattern began to emerge. Lorenzo Calbretti had uncovered

The Italian Vineyard Mystery

a web of deceit, a conspiracy that reached far beyond petty theft. He had stumbled upon something dark, something dangerous, and he had been silenced for it.

"He knew," Antonio whispered, his eyes fixed on the page, his voice hoarse with emotion. "My father knew he was in danger. He wrote about threats, about men following him, about being afraid for his life."

The oppressive atmosphere of the North field intensified, closing in on them like a suffocating blanket. The air grew heavy, filled with the weight of unspoken words and unanswered questions.

Suddenly, Merlin stiffened, his ears pricked, a low growl rumbling in his chest. He moved closer to Eliza, his body tense, his eyes fixed on something beyond the veil of tangled vines.

"What is it, Merlin?" Eliza whispered, her hand instinctively going to his soft fur. "What do you see?"

Before Merlin could react further, a voice, sliced through the silence.

"Well, well, well... look what we have here."

Eliza and Antonio whirled around to face the source of the voice. Standing at the edge of the clearing, her arms crossed, a cruel smile playing on his lips, stood Illya, the riding instructor. But something about her demeanor had changed. Gone was the façade of quiet competence, replaced by an aura of cold menace.

"Illya?" Antonio said, "What are you doing here?"

Illya laughed, a harsh, grating sound that echoed through the stillness of the neglected vineyard.

"What does it look like, Antonio?" she sneered, taking a step closer. "I'm here to tie up loose ends."

．．．

Her hand darted into the folds of her riding jacket, and for a moment, Eliza thought she might pull out a weapon. Instead, she withdrew a small brass key. It glinted in the dappled sunlight. It was Lorenzo's.

"You," Antonio breathed, his voice a mixture of anger and disbelief. "It was you all along. We've been looking for that key. Papa wore it on neck all the time."

Illya's lips curled into a cruel smile. "You were always a fool, Antonio," she spat. "Too blinded by your own naiveté to see what was right in front of you. Give me my stipend or your waters will all be poisoned."

"Why?" Antonio choked out, his voice thick with emotion. "Why would you do this?"

Eliza gripped Antonio's hand. "What is the key for?"

"Our irrigation system. It goes to all the plants."

Illya's eyes glittered with a mixture of hatred and something else, something colder and more calculating.

"Because your father was weak," she sang out. "He was too busy clinging to his precious traditions, too afraid to embrace change, to see that he needed to leave Francesca."

"He loved this vineyard," Antonio whispered, his voice breaking. "He dedicated his life to it. And you will ruin it with one fell swoop?"

"And look where it got him," Illya sneered. "Dead and buried, with nothing but a legacy of lies."

She took a step closer, her face contorted in a mask of rage. "I did what I had to do," she hissed. "Your father was in the way, clinging to the past. It was time for a new era, a Calbretti vineyard ruled by someone with vision, with ambition. The vines die or else."

"You won't get away with this," Antonio said, his voice low and dangerous. "My father kept a journal. He wrote everything down. People know what you did."

The Italian Vineyard Mystery

Illya's smile widened, becoming almost predatory. "Do they now?" she purred. "And who do you think they'll believe? The grieving son, blinded by grief and rage, passed over by his own father, or a respected member of the community with nothing but the vineyard's best interests at heart like the Rizzo's?"

She took another step closer, her gaze locking with Antonio's. "You see, Antonio," she whispered, her voice like silk over steel, "in the end, it's all about perception. And I control the narrative."

Eliza knew they were in grave danger. Illya was unhinged, consumed by her own ambition and twisted sense of justice. She had already killed once; she wouldn't hesitate to do it again. They needed to get out of there, to get help.

Thinking fast, Eliza reached out and subtly nudged Antonio, signaling him to distract Illya while she made a run for it. She knew that if she could reach the main road, she could get help.

Antonio, sensing her intentions, took a step forward, putting himself between Eliza and Illya.

"This isn't over, Illya," he said, his voice low and steady, but Eliza could see the fear in his eyes.

"Oh, but it is, Antonio," Illya said, her smile turning feral. "It is over. For you, at least."

She lunged at Antonio, her hands outstretched, and for a moment, time seemed to slow to a crawl. Eliza's breath caught in her throat as she braced herself for the impact, but it never came.

There was a blur of orange, a flash of teeth, and a startled yelp. Merlin, with a fierce growl threw himself at Illya.

Chapter Fourteen

The world around them erupted into chaos. Illya stumbled back, her expression shifting from surprise to fury as Merlin's powerful form collided with her midsection, knocking her off balance. The brass key clattered to the earth, rolling away into the shadows of the twisted vines and piles of leaves. Antonio seized the moment, shouting, "Eliza, go!"

But she hesitated, torn by the need to help and the urgency to escape.

"Eliza!" Antonio's voice cut through her hesitation, sharp as glass. "Now!"

Merlin had managed to hold Illya distracted, his powerful, fierce growl echoing through the field, but she was regaining her footing. The wild, primal fear in his eyes mirrored Eliza's own rising panic. Eliza knew they only had moments.

The Italian Vineyard Mystery

. . .

With a newfound resolve, Eliza turned and sprinted towards the edge of the field, weaving through the overgrown weeds and branches. Every thump of her heart echoed the breathless urgency of their situation. She could hear the struggle behind her—the harsh voices and the snarls. The world blurred as she ran, instinct taking over, focused solely on escape.

Then, as if the very air were alive with danger, she heard a strangled cry—a desperate plea mingled with a deep, resonant growl.

Terror gripped her stomach like a vice. She stumbled but regained her momentum, pushing through the feeling of dread that threatened to consume her. It was no longer just about her survival; the sound of Antonio's voice, however distant, called her back. She needed to help him.

But the world had transformed around her. The North field was a labyrinth of shadows, the fading light morphed the twisted vines into gnarled hands reaching out for her. Each step felt heavier, weighed down by the dark secrets they'd unearthed. She could not leave Antonio behind; nor Merlin. She wouldn't let them face Illya alone.

She skidded to a halt, breathless, and turned back. From the crooked expanse of the field, she spotted them—Antonio, now on the ground, grappling with Illya who, fueled by fury and desperation, fought like a woman possessed.

The key lay forgotten on the ground, somewhere, hidden in the dusky light. Eliza's instincts screamed at her to act. She rushed towards where she thought it had fallen, plunging her hand into the dirt, scraping through the leaves. Finally she grabbed the brass key, feeling its cold weight settle into her palm. In that moment, a surge of determination ignited within her. This key represented not just a literal unlocking but a chance to reclaim the Calbretti's hope.

"Eliza, watch out!" Antonio drew her attention back to the violent struggle unfolding before her. Illya's grasp was tightening around Antonio's throat, her face twisted in a mask of rage. Merlin rode the woman's back, high up near her shoulders.

Eliza gritted her teeth and steadied herself. She wasn't about to let fear anchor her down. With renewed vigor, she sprinted toward them, the brass key clutched tightly in her hand.

"Illya!" she yelled, her voice rising above the chaos. "You're finished. This ends now!"

Illya's head snapped towards Eliza, her eyes widening in shock and disbelief at the sight of the key. In that split

The Italian Vineyard Mystery

second, she loosened her grip on Antonio just enough for him to wriggle free, gasping for breath.

"You don't understand what you're meddling with!" Illya hissed, her composure cracking amid the chaos. "You think you can just waltz in here and claim what doesn't belong to you?"

Eliza planted her feet. "This vineyard belongs to Antonio. It's his heritage, not yours to steal! If you think manipulation and deceit can create a future, you're mistaken."

Illya's eyes narrowed, boiling in fury. "Your impudence will cost you dearly." She briefly took a step back to regain her footing and tried to get Merlin off of her.

Without thinking, Eliza raised the key, the fading sunlight catching its metallic sheen. "This is the key to the irrigation system, Illya—the lifeblood of the vineyard. And I will use it to expose the truth about you and your crimes! We will ensure the truth is known."

With a fierce rallying cry, she threw herself to the side, intercepting Illya's planned charge with a swing of the key. It struck against the nearest cypress tree, making a loud clamor that stopped Illya in her tracks. The sound reverberated throughout the field, a sharp reminder of the stakes at play.

. . .

"Back off, Illya!" Antonio shouted, now regaining his strength. He pushed himself up, wiping the dirt off his face.

Illya glanced between them, calculating her next move. The mercurial glint in her eyes betrayed her unease. "You think you can challenge me? I've built my life around power, while you've clung to illusions! Why else would I be fucking such an old man?"

"Illusions?" Eliza whispered incredulously. "The love for family, the truth of our heritage? Those aren't illusions, Illya. They are the roots of what this vineyard stands for. And you're trying to poison it!"

Illya lashed out angrily, "You know nothing! You are an outsider."

Antonio stepped forward, his voice steady and firm. "We know enough. You destroyed my father, and now you want to destroy this place because of your greed. You'll pay for your crimes."

Merlin positioned himself protectively beside Eliza, his low growl rising again, reaffirming their united stance.

. . .

The Italian Vineyard Mystery

Illya headed for the cypress tree. Antonio tackled her and Merlin joined in while Eliza went to hunt for the key one more time.

"Keep her down," Eliza yelled. She thrust her feet through the vegetation and got onto her hands and knees until she saw the key again.

"Got it." By now Antonio had Illya's arms pinned behind her.

"Go get help," he said.

Merlin turned to Eliza. "Let me go. I'm faster. Put me on the horse."

"You sure?" Eliza asked.

"I've watched you all these years."

Eliza found the mare grazing two rows over. "Sorry girl. We need you." She plucked her cat up and put him on the saddle and loosely tied the reins, then aimed the horse for the main complex and clucked and waved her hands.

"Be careful, Merlin!" she cried as the horse cantered home.

Chapter Fifteen

The roar of the ATV engine sliced through the morning quiet, echoing off the centuries-old olive trees that lined the dusty path. Guilia clung tightly to Inspector Mario as they bounced and jolted along, the urgency of the situation lending an edge to the crisp air. They rounded a bend and burst onto a scene of utter chaos.

Antonio, his face contorted with fury and exertion, held a struggling figure on the ground. Dust billowed around them, kicked up by the frantic movements of the woman pinned beneath Antonio's powerful grip. As Guilia and Inspector Mario skidded to a stop, Antonio looked up, his voice hoarse with triumph and barely controlled rage.

"We found the killer!"

Inspector Mario wasted no time. He leapt from the ATV, Guilia hot on his heels. As they neared the struggling pair, Guilia gasped. It was Illya, his eyes wild with. She thrashed violently under Antonio's hold, her face contorted in a snarl.

Eliza knelt beside the struggling pair, her gaze sharp

The Italian Vineyard Mystery

and assessing. Illya's jacket, torn in the struggle, had fallen open, revealing its lining. It was a deep crimson, woven through with delicate threads of gold, glinting in the sunlight. Her breath caught in her throat as recognition slammed into her, cold and swift.

"That's it," she breathed, her voice trembling slightly. "That's the same thread."

The others stared at her, their faces etched with confusion.

"The same thread from the murder scene," she clarified, her eyes locked on the luxurious fabric. "Fine silk, woven with gold. It's rare, expensive. I remember thinking it was strange to see it on a work jacket."

Antonio's grip on Illya tightened a fraction, his face hardening into an implacable mask. "You're sure?"

Eliza nodded, her gaze never wavering. "I'm sure."

With a decisive movement, Inspector Mario pulled out a pair of handcuffs and secured Illya's wrists. Illya, defeated, stopped struggling. She glared at them all, her gaze venomous, but she remained silent.

"We'll take her to the station," Inspector Mario barked, his voice ringing with authority. "She'll be charged with murder."

As two officers, arriving in response to Inspector Mario's call, bundled a cuffed and seething Illya into the back of their patrol car, a heavy silence descended upon the group. The dust settled, leaving behind a palpable tension in its wake although Eliza thought she'd taste that dust for days.

Eliza, Merlin, and Antonio made their way back to the main house, each lost in their own thoughts. The air, thick with the scent of olive groves and the receding echo of the ATV engine. Francesca sat on the veranda, her face showing her concern. When she saw them approaching, a flicker of hope lit up her eyes, quickly replaced by an anxious frown.

Antonio, his usual swagger subdued, was the first to speak. He told his mother everything, recounting the events of the morning with a quiet intensity that betrayed the turmoil brewing within him.

Francesca listened intently, her expression a canvas of shifting emotions—relief, anger, sadness, and finally, a steely resolve. When Antonio finished, she reached out and took his hand, her touch conveying a depth of understanding that transcended words.

"You did well, Antonio," she said, her voice firm. "You brought justice for your father."

Antonio nodded, accepting her praise with a somber nod. His eyes, however, were fixed on Eliza, a silent question burning in their depths.

"We have to leave in the morning," Eliza said softly, her voice laced with regret. "Our flight is early."

Antonio's face fell, his disappointment palpable. He nodded slowly, understanding in his eyes.

"I understand," he said quietly. "But this isn't over. We'll deal with the Rizzos." His voice hardened, the vow laced with a chilling promise.

Eliza placed a hand on his arm, her touch gentle. "Antonio," she said softly, "vengeance won't bring your father back. Let the law run its course."

He looked at her, his gaze searching hers, then nodded slowly. He knew she was right, but the need for justice, for something more than just legal retribution, burned fiercely within him.

The following morning dawned bright and clear, the sun casting a golden glow over the olive groves. The beauty

The Italian Vineyard Mystery

of the day seemed at odds with the somber mood that had settled over the estate. After heartfelt goodbyes and promises to stay in touch, Eliza and Merlin climbed into the waiting car, the driver holding the door open for them.

As the car pulled away, Eliza looked back at Antonio, who stood silently on the veranda, his mother by his side. Their eyes met one last time, a silent acknowledgment of the bond forged in the midst of tragedy. Then, with a sigh, Eliza turned away, her gaze fixed on the road ahead, her mind already awhirl with tasks that awaited her back in New York. Days turned into weeks as Eliza settled back into her routine, the bustling streets of New York contrasting sharply with the tranquil olive groves of Siena. But the memories lingered, haunting her thoughts as she sifted through waves of paperwork at her desk. And finally, she did receive her invitation to The Society of Fabric Specialists, which she gladly accepted.

Two months later, Eliza was pleasantly surprised to get a text from Antonio.

We got the Rizzos to pay us back. My father's book proved they'd stolen some of our stock. They'd been selling our wines under an illegal label. The Association was going to ban them but we worked out a compromise.

I miss you, dear Eliza.

I don't miss Merlin.

The End

Note to the reader: Kindly leave a review if so inspired. And read the next book when Eliza and Merlin take on Vienna!

Printed in Great Britain
by Amazon